Warner Bros.

A Warner Communications Company

First Artists

presents

A Sweetwall Production
in association with
Casablanca Filmworks

DUSTIN HOFFMAN   VANESSA REDGRAVE

in

AGATHA

Also Starring

Timothy Dalton

Helen Morse

Screenplay by Kathleen Tynan and
Arthur Hopcraft

Produced by Jarvis Astaire and Gavrik Losey

Directed by Michael Apted

AGATHA

by Kathleen Tynan

BALLANTINE BOOKS · NEW YORK

Library of Congress Catalog Card Number: 78-17508

ISBN 0-345-27586-1

Manufactured in the United States of America

First Edition: August 1978

Paperback Format
First Edition: September 1978

First U.S. Printing: April 1979

To Ken

On December 4, 1926, the famous mystery writer Agatha Christie disappeared from her home. So began a strange episode that has never been convincingly explained. What follows is an imaginary solution to an authentic mystery.

Chapter 1

It was the morning of December 2, 1926, and the kitchen clock at Styles, in the village of Sunningdale, read nine-fifteen. Jane, the parlormaid, who was something of a pedant, nudged the butler. "Time to fetch the car," she said. The butler finished his tea in his own time, then went out to the garage. He started the ignition of the bottle-nosed Morris and reversed the car into the driveway.

The house, like the car, spoke comfortable affluence. A large Neo-Tudor building of red brick and black beams, high chimneys and small latticed windows, it stood in an acre of garden. The garden in turn was surrounded by tall and somber pines. Smoke puffed through a high chimney stack. The butler snapped a dead head off a winter rosebush and went back inside.

A tall woman came out of the front door. She wore a slim-fitting coat with a fur collar pulled up against the cold. She waited by the door of the car, her breath standing on the December air, and looked up at the house. She had red hair, a fair complexion, and a beautiful face of a particularly English gentility. She was thirty-six years old, and it was the first morning in six months that she had cared to be alive.

Five minutes went by but Agatha Christie showed no signs of impatience. Two more minutes passed before a handsome man of thirty-seven, Col. Archibald Christie, slammed the front door of the house behind him and climbed into the passenger seat of the car. He wore his fair brown hair and his moustache clipped, and he was dressed for his office in the City of London. His good looks were of the kind that illustrate cigarette advertisements and army recruiting posters.

The car traveled through the affluent village, past grotesque imitation Tudor and Gothic dwellings recently built to house army officers and colonial administrators no longer required to run the shrinking British Empire. Back they came from abroad to new settlements like Sunningdale, a mere hour from their London clubs, to stake out their day with golf and bridge rather than military parades and the government of the conquered. At home they had to make do with three servants rather than a hundred.

Both Agatha and Archie Christie came from the officer class—Agatha on her mother's side. Her father, a congenial American with a small inheritance, had embraced a lifetime of leisure without qualms. His daughter approved his lack of ambition.

Archie Christie, on the other hand, whose father had been an official in the Indian Civil Service, who himself had won countless medals in the war and returned to England a hero, felt—as did his mother and young brother and almost everybody else in Sunningdale—that postwar life had short-changed him.

Unlike his peers, however, who thought commerce disreputable, Archie earned a living in the world of finance.

His wife, too, earned a living, although she thought that writing highly successful detective fiction was a game, a hobby, like embroidery, to occupy the hours when her husband took to the golf course; that it was a diversion from the real business of life, which was her marriage and her child. Until recently, she had confidently expected to be happy forever.

Agatha Christie emerged from a Devonshire childhood—which was privileged although remote from the center of things, where she had been cocooned by a loving mother and by long hours of daydreaming—and stood shyly on the threshold of life to await what nursemaids and governesses then called her fate. Many different types of young men came her way, encountered riding, in Paris, at weekend houseparties, on the dance floor, during a winter season in Cairo. Then she fell in love. Archibald Christie was tall, blue-eyed, and his own man. When war was declared, they were separated. Agatha nursed the wounded; Archie, a soldier by profession, transferred to the Royal Flying Corps and returned from abroad with the Commander of St. Michael and St. George, the

Distinguished Service Order, one or two other medals, and mention in five military dispatches. They set up house and had a daughter and lived happily till twelve years later, when the marriage lay ruptured and bleeding. During the previous summer, soon after the death of Agatha's mother, Archie had told her that he had fallen in love with another woman.

There is nothing like being behind the wheel of a motor car on a fine day to persuade the driver that life is manageable. On this Thursday morning in December, Agatha felt confident that all would be well, that the bad times would end, that she had fully recovered from the nervous breakdown brought on by her mother's death and her husband's defection. When Archie laughed at the angle of her hat and stroked her nose in an old familiar way, she smiled like a child welcomed back to grace. Archie had all the confidence of a man without imagination. He had no need of it; his class, his great good looks and athletic body guaranteed him success. He was, in his own fashion, impregnable.

Agatha drove her car into the station yard and parked it. Her husband jumped out, made a cursory gesture to open his wife's door, and turned toward the station.

He handed his ticket to the collector and led his wife through to the platform.

"That's where he did it." Agatha pointed to the rail line. "That little man in the white house down the road from us. Knelt down there and put his head on the tracks as the train came in."

"Showy way to kill yourself," Archie said. "I wonder why.

"You should use it," he added, mildly condescending. "You usually do. Nice bit of action to get your teeth into."

"I don't like messy deaths," she said and tucked her hand more firmly under Archie's arm. She was pleased out of proportion when the station-master greeted them, as each day he did. "Colonel Christie, good morning. Good morning, ma'am." Agatha relished the comforting anonymity of belonging to Archie. She looked up at her husband.

"Do you think it's going to be all right? I woke up this morning feeling that if I could be buoyant again, if I could make you laugh . . . Ever since Mother died I've been no fun at all, Archie. I'm so sorry."

He smiled slightly and continued in the direction of the tunnel leading to the opposite platform. "You've got to get well."

She looked at him. "If only your life weren't so . . ."

"Squalid?" he asked.

A piercing whistle cut her reply. As the train came into view Archie suddenly turned toward the rails and, to reach the other side, bounded confidently across the tracks, perilously close to the oncoming engine. Agatha's view of him was blocked by the stationary train. When it pulled out she stood for some minutes on the platform and wept.

Mr. Gilling had been in charge of the Sunning-dale pharmacy since the building of the railway in the 1850's. The colored glass jars and old-fashioned pharmaceutical bottles showed his fingerprints on layers of dust. He mixed prescriptions these days as cavalierly as a practiced conjuror. He had not lost enthusiasm and always produced a satisfactory result. An amateur of murder mysteries, he'd read all Mrs. Christie's books and he liked nothing better than a specialized chat with his local celebrity. Agatha presented him with a prescription for a sleeping draught.

"I have that empty bottle of hyoscyamine for you." She looked at him blankly. "You wanted it for the cover of a book. Had it here for weeks." Agatha took the bottle from him and examined it carefully.

"I do care how my books look," she said and Mr. Gilling nodded. "I'd never commit suicide by any other means than hyoscyamine."

"Quite right," Mr. Gilling said, "though if you wished to avoid detection, a slow poisoning by arsenic would be favorable."

"Like Charles Bravo?" Agatha smiled. "The most baffling of all the unsolved cases, in my view. Was it antimony, do you think? I'm inclined to the view that he took the poison himself."

"In my view, it was the doctor who was responsible."

"Have you ever had the urge to poison anyone, Mr. Gilling?"

"Good gracious, Mrs. Christie!"

"Of course you haven't."

The chemist nodded. "Well, you're looking much better," he said inconsequentially.

Agatha smiled.

"And your daughter?"

"Is extremely well."

"And the dog?"

"'Tiptop, Mr. Gilling," she said.

People in the village knew Mrs. Christie had had her troubles.

She got into her car and settled into her own recent habit of loneliness, exhausted by the chemist, by her effort at affability. The morning had not held to its promise. She called up memories on which she depended for a lifeline, childhood memories of Devon, her beloved nurse, her mother on a sunlit lawn, skating on the ice rink in Torquay, embroidering huge bunches of clematis on a cushion cover. But anxious scenarios intruded: the death of her father when she was eleven; her mother's grief at the loss of him. Now, her own fear of loss. And her mother was no longer there to comfort and succor her.

Agatha started her car and drove toward home. As she turned a corner a dog darted in front of her and she braked, swerving across the road. In her mind's eye the dog she had narrowly missed became her old childhood pet who had been knocked down in a Devon lane. She had found him, fixed a scarf around his wound, and carried him gently home to her mother. Her mother knew what to do. She had always known the answers.

A policeman tapped the window of her car, then opened the door. "I don't know what you think you're doing, madam," he told her, "but your car's blocking the road." Agatha looked at him blankly. "Name and license, please."

She stared at the man and could not remember her name. She was shaking with fear. She opened her handbag and found the license and handed it over. The young man examined it. He saw how frightened the woman looked and took pity. "Mrs. Christie, I suggest you take a little more care in future."

He handed the license back and Agatha drove off toward Styles.

At the door to meet her was Charlotte Fisher, the daughter of a Scottish rector. A large girl in her late twenties, pleasantly plain, Miss Fisher had come to work as both governess to the Christies' daughter, Rosalind, and secretary to Agatha. She also acted as friend, confidante, and surrogate mother.

"Mr. Collins telephoned," she said, helping her employer off with her coat. "He offered to send a car but I said you'd drive yourself to London." She followed Agatha through the paneled hall to the study.

"He knows I haven't written a word for months."

"Well, I told him you'd finished a story."

Agatha smiled. "That won't help, Charlotte. What will you say next week?" She searched through her desk, picked up some typed sheets, a pile of press clippings, some newspaper photographs of herself. Under her typewriter she found a pack of paper strips held together with a rubber band. She examined them, wrote ANTIMONY in large letters at the top of one bit of paper, shuffled the pieces together, and replaced the band.

She looked around her at the small models of

animals from South Africa, bought with Archie on their trip around the world. She took in the bookshelves, the fringed lampshades, the water colors of Egypt, the photographs of her eight-year-old daughter and of many family dogs. The room no longer reassured her. Charlotte watched her mistress as if at any moment she might do something irregular.

Agatha suddenly laughed. "Don't stand there like a jailer. I'm not going to froth at the mouth or go berserk. Look at your feet, Charlotte, they're worse than mine."

Charlotte looked down in some surprise at her lisle stockings and comfortable flat shoes.

"Not the shoes," Agatha continued. "It's what's in them. Your feet don't caper. You should come to my dancing lessons. Probably cheer you up more than they do me."

"I don't know what you're going on about, Agatha," Miss Fisher said. "And it's time you got ready. Mr. Collins said half London would be out to honor you."

"Publisher's stuff," said her mistress. "Writers in need of a free meal. Archie said he'd turn up, but I don't know. He'll hate it. Wish it was just him and me, though I daresay I'm not much fun at the moment."

Charlotte summoned her courage. "Don't show him what you feel. It frightens him."

"How can I not show what I feel to the person I'm closest to? You simply don't understand."

"No, I don't. But people change. You may no longer suit."

"We were never suited, Charlotte. Our tastes were always different."

"Like golf."

"Yes, like golf and lots of other things. But we built up a bond. You can't just change that, like ordering up a new tonic. If the bond breaks you have to put it together again. There's no other solution. That's what I'm going to do." She moved two Staffordshire dogs into line on the mantelpiece, then turned to her secretary.

"Is he spending next weekend with Nancy?"

Miss Fisher, who was not a shirker, nodded. "I imagine so."

"If he'd only take *me* away."

"You went away. That didn't work. You can't ask the Colonel for help. He's your . . . He's your . . . adversary."

A

At the door of an imposing Edwardian club in Pall Mall, fifty or more people pushed forward to present their tickets and be admitted. They made up the last of a crowd of some four hundred people come to honor Agatha Christie at the expense of her publisher, William Collins.

Some latecomers fared better than others. Wally Stanton paid his cab, adjusted the brim of his Dobbs hat, and entered the club, where he was immediately recognized. The hat he wore had appeared that month in *Vanity Fair*, was the height of fashion in New York; yet it sat perfectly easily on Wally Stanton, who came from Loveland, Colorado, a forgettable town in the foothills of the Rockies. Wally was short, neat, and elegant. He sat comfortably in himself as well as in his clothes. He was also gracefully diligent, and had in his youth delivered mail, cut hay, sold groceries, and, one winter, walked ten miles in a temperature of forty below to teach Aristotle's *Poetics* to a class of high school students. His mother, a poor English immigrant, made him read Milton, Tom Paine, and the Bible, and told her academic son that the world was his. While her son Wally worked his way through college, her husband mismanaged the homestead; her elder son, Aaron, took to the bottle, fell down a flight of stairs and died in a pool of vomit. But Wally made good. He wrote for the *Loveland Reporter,* then moved to the *Denver Post.* Along with many a bright-eyed lad he dreamed of New York. "When are you going to get to the big town?" his friends asked. He said, "I'll go there." And he did. Now, at the age of forty, he was half persuaded that there was nothing more a poor boy could ask than to become a successful journalist, half convinced that his brother, Aaron, had been the poet of the family and made the right choice.

Wally Stanton had been in London for six months, on loan from the Hearst Newspapers to the *Globe-Enquirer.* The owner of the *Globe,* a British peer much impressed by the methods of transatlantic journalism and particularly by Stanton's lively style, had hired him on contract to fill the gossip column. Since other successful gossip columnists of the day were titled, almost to a man, Lord Dintworth thought it amusing to open closed doors to an outsider. Stanton's weekly column proved unpredictable, even outrageous, and often funny. He used being an American to infiltrate, to shock, and to surprise, and he reported what was new from across the seas. His English readers thought him very amusing; he allowed them to laugh at him.

As Wally was being greeted by an official of Collins publishing house, John Foster was being given the cold shoulder. The reporter from the *Sunningdale Echo* had counted on easy access. But the official said his ticket was not in order, nor his mode of dress. Foster protested without effect. He was neither fleet nor cunning, but a young man with a kind heart and poor co-ordination. His father, a retired batman in the Indian army, thought his son half-witted and lucky enough to even work for a newspaper.

"You see," said Foster, "Mrs. Christie's our local celebrity. They'd fire me if I missed this."

"John Foster!" interrupted Wally Stanton. "Good to see you." He turned to the official. "He's with me."

The reporter from the *Sunningdale Echo* blinked. The official changed his tune. Wally gave Foster a little nudge to get him to move, and in they went.

Foster said, "Foster's the name. Very good of you, Mr. Stanton. I never miss your column."

Archibald Christie fared less well than John Foster. He had forgotten his ticket to the lunch in honor of his wife, had not wished in the first place to be there, and lost his temper at the treatment he received on arrival. A higher-up was sent for.

A man in a loud check suit said, without enthusiasm, "Can I help you?"

"I'm looking for my wife," Christie replied through clenched teeth.

"Oh, yes?"

"Archibald Christie."

The brash-looking man was instantly accommodating. "Oh, you're the husband. Come this way."

Along a balcony above the great oval well of the building, William Collins edged forward his famous author.

"I'm terrified, Mr. Collins. You have no idea how bad I am at this. Never again."

"These things can be awfully helpful, my dear."

She shuddered. "Locked up with four hundred people in that room. I should write about it. I'm the victim and everyone else is somehow implicated in my death."

"And then?"

"Hm. A verbal trick, perhaps. A girl's name that turns out to belong to a boy? Four hundred murderers, a bit much don't you think? But I could take on a dozen." She looked down nervously at the crowd below. "Or could I?"

Collins smiled. "You look awfully pretty today."

"Archie says I look appalling."

"Then, my dear," said her publisher, "you must look quite wonderful in normal circumstances."

"My secretary told you I'd finished that story. I haven't, I'm afraid. Ending's not right. That pompous little Poirot, I made it too easy for him."

Collins said, "Why not make him the murderer?"

"Over my dead body!" She laughed, and together they walked down the spiral staircase into the crowd.

The celebrity of the day attracted no attention. Her good looks were disguised by a matronly dress and an unbecoming hat. She looked anxiously for her husband, whose height and presence always turned heads. The sight of him there made her feel joyfully assured; as with an addict, this pleasure always blocked the promise of pain.

Collins followed Agatha to Archie's side. "So good to see you," he said. "We're frightfully proud of her, y'know. Beaten all the records with this one."

The official who had allowed Archie in asked if he might have a word with Collins, and Agatha was left smiling at her husband. She said, "I'm so glad—"

"Who is that dreadful little man?" her husband interrupted. "Suit with huge squares and cufflinks the size of manholes."

Agatha laughed. "I don't know. I'm so happy you came."

Collins signaled for them to follow and they moved into the vast Edwardian dining room to the top table, where many introductions were made and praises lavished on the author whose concern was only for Archie. It occurred to her that such immoderate love of her husband must be a punishable vice.

Behind the top table a large banner illustrated the cover of the latest Christie success: *The Murder of Roger Ackroyd.* A profile of a man at one end faced a profile of a woman at the other. Copies of the book lay in piles around the room.

Wally Stanton, his unlikely luncheon partner from Sunningdale at his side, sat just below the top table and observed the literary scene with growing boredom. He glanced at the guest list that Collins had seen fit to give him and marked a few names. Several guests were brought over to be introduced to Wally, and each in turn smiled fawningly upon him in the hope of a mention in his column. John Foster was impressed. This was only the second time that the editor of the *Echo* had allowed him to cover a story outside Sunningdale. He took elaborate notes, slicked back his fair hair from time to time, and drank too much brandy. At the age of twenty-six he felt that his world was in blossom.

He pointed out Mrs. Christie to Wally. "She must be pleased as punch," he said. Wally thought the celebrity sitting just above them at the top table looked remarkably unhappy. "That's her husband on the left of her," John said. "He's a very fine golfer is the Colonel."

"I bet," Wally said. "Doesn't look as if he's enjoying the literary world."

"You know, she's come under a lot of fire for this book. Her Watson turns out to be the murderer. The experts think that's cheating. It's worried me a great deal, to tell you the truth, Mr. Stanton."

Wally nodded politely. Murder hardly seemed the province of the sad-looking woman on the platform.

During the course of the lunch he noticed that Colonel Christie neither smiled at nor talked to his wife. When she touched him once to get his attention, he ignored her.

After coffee and brandy had been served, William Collins, who sat on Agatha's left, rose, tapped his glass with his fork, and silenced the room.

"I should like to say how proud we are to have attracted so many distinguished members of the literary world and, above all, how proud I am to be sitting next to this charming lady. We captured her this year and she rewarded us with this classic of crime. We apparently have rewarded her with a new greenhouse. Quite evidently, the house of Collins got the better deal."

The room laughed. Wally noticed that while Collins spoke, Colonel Christie was busy trying to attract the attention of a waiter.

The publisher continued. *"The Murder of Roger Ackroyd* is, in my entirely unbiased view"— he paused for the laughter—"her best book. Yet everything she's written since *The Mysterious Affair at Styles,* which was published six years ago, has been of exceptional quality. Mrs. Christie has rapidly joined the very best detective writers of her generation. Today I'm going to tell you something about her. As she is the least vain and most private of my authors, I found my researches singularly difficult. Nonetheless, as an amateur sleuth and with Mrs. Christie's unwilling cooperation, I am going to divulge a few secrets, some information about the lady which may throw some light on her work.

"She is the youngest child of Frederick and Clara Miller, and was brought up in a large villa in Torquay. The fashionable resort suited her father, an American, a companionable man much liked by all who knew him, who became a patron of the local cricket club. Now, Mrs. Miller was a woman of independent ideas. She sent her eldest daughter to boarding school. But by the time her youngest child was born her views on education had radically changed. She was convinced that no child should learn to read till the age of eight, and that the best thing for her daughter was to let her amuse herself. The results were salutary. Mrs. Miller, I presume, was an inspired story-teller. And so addicted was her highly imaginative daughter that before the age of five she had taught herself to read. Here was a crook opening a safe. A mathematician solving a problem. With the help of her innocent nurse, who read to her from picture books, the young Agatha memorized words till she could fit them into the puzzle.

"Later on, there were piano lessons, dancing lessons, lessons in mathematics from her father. But no school. Instead, long blissful hours of play with imaginary friends. Miss Miller had her secrets. Things since then have hardly changed. Mrs. Christie certainly gives us information, but in such a cunning fashion that very few of us ever guess the solution to her mysteries."

The audience applauded.

"She completed her exceptionally happy if somewhat unusual education at the Paris Conservatoire. There she learned to sing and play the piano. Fortunately, nerves overcame her at the keyboard and she abandoned the idea of becoming a professional.

"How and when, then, did pen reach paper?

Mrs. Christie began to read the works of Sherlock Holmes, which had much the same effect that sitting under an apple tree had upon Newton."

The audience laughed and Collins continued.

"Incidentally, Mrs. Christie usually solves her plots while chewing on an apple in her bath. Make of that what you will."

Agatha smiled up at her publisher, while her husband stared stonily ahead.

"Our plot now thickens. Her sister challenged her to try her hand at a detective story, and some years later, while working in a dispensary, she began *The Mysterious Affair at Styles*. I have one more secret for you. Mrs. Christie considered herself then, as she does now, to be an amateur, a dabbler in the art of fiction. Not only do her books disprove such a theory; so, indeed, does the lady herself. She is a stickler for detail. Some time ago, she told me—with a firmness I hardly expected from so gentle a creature—that she didn't want her sentences edited. 'I don't want them made more grammatical,' she said, 'when they are part of someone's spoken conversation.' How right she was. And just as she protects her written word, so she cares for the design of the jacket and all the other small details that make a good book. I applaud her professionalism and I respect it.

"Her first novel gave birth to a small Belgian retired police officer with a formidable number of 'little grey cells of the mind.' Ladies and gentlemen, I ask you to rise and drink a toast to Hercule Poirot and his brilliant inventor."

Calls for "speech" and "author" followed Collins's address. Agatha rose, said "Thank you" almost inaudibly, and sat down.

Her publisher jumped up again. "Roger Ackroyd and his famous creator have one thing in common. Their lips are sealed. Mrs. Christie agreed to be seen here today but refuses to be heard." He leaned down and whispered something in Agatha's ear. Then he continued. "However, my friends, should you wish to receive a signed copy of her book, Mrs. Christie will be delighted to oblige."

The luncheon tables began to break up. William Collins led Agatha down off the platform and seated her at a table piled high with copies of *The Murder of Roger Ackroyd*. While she signed her book, and at Agatha's request, he endeavored to amuse Archie Christie. Wally Stanton made a casual round of the room, asked a few questions, took some notes, introduced his Sunningdale acolyte to one or two writers.

Outside the club, in Pall Mall, a crowd of around forty people was being held back by police. Most of those waiting to see the celebrity were conspicuously poor, the men among them evidently unemployed. They watched the exodus from the lunch with unsmiling curiosity.

Wally walked out and stood watching the crowd with an outsider's interest. He was followed shortly by Agatha and Archie with William Collins. No one recognized the star of the afternoon. Collins got into his car. "I'll telephone you," he said. Agatha smiled and waved as her publisher was driven off. Wally moved closer to Agatha and Archie, who stood waiting for their car.

"Can't think why you wore a black dress," Archie said to his wife. "You can't go on wearing mourning forever."

"Well, I just thought it looked nice." She stroked her husband's arm, which he abruptly withdrew. "Why don't you like me touching you?"

"I don't mind."

"I'm so grateful you came," she said.

He looked away from her and said, "I found it all rather insulting. That reference to your buying the greenhouse. I've really had enough of all this. These people. Your writing. Your damned garden. I'm simply not my own person any more."

"Please, darling, let's talk about it in the car."

"I'll walk to the office," her husband said and moved off at speed.

Agatha got into her car and drove south toward the river, then along Fleet Street, by St. Paul's and into the City, past men in top hats and wing collars with flushed postprandial faces returning unwillingly to their desks. Opposite a tall building in Leadenhall Street Agatha parked her car. Once or twice while waiting there, she looked into the driving mirror. She took off her hat and half-heartedly arranged her short hair. The man in the news stall beside her car blew on his fingers, then uncurled himself from his stall and offered Agatha a copy of the evening paper. Its banner headline read: MINERS BACK AT WORK. SEVEN-MONTH "HOLIDAY" OVER. She rolled down her window and paid the news vendor.

"It's all over now," he said, pushing the paper through the window. "They're bringing home less than they made before the strike. Goes to show you, doesn't it?" Agatha nodded and rolled up the window.

She saw her husband get out of a taxi and bound up the steps of his office with that familiar grace that turned her heart. Without thought, she followed him into the building, up three flights of steps to a door marked "Empire Developments (London) Inc."

Agatha told the receptionist to let her husband know she wished to see him. The receptionist smiled a careful smile and made to pick up the telephone on her desk. Then she changed her mind and said, "If you'll kindly wait, Mrs. Christie."

A minute or two later the woman reappeared and led Agatha to her husband's office. It was a modest room with leather armchairs and a photograph of a fighter plane. A map indicated in red that most of the world still belonged to the British. As Agatha entered, a young woman of around twenty-five stood up. She had alabaster skin, dark hair, and a full, pretty figure. Miss Nancy Neele was placidly appealing.

"I told your husband you were here but he said he was terribly busy and would you like to leave a message with me?"

Agatha faced her opponent with resolve.

"No, I'd rather like to speak to him myself."

The Colonel's secretary began to sort some papers on the desk. "That's what I told him," she said, "but he's waiting for the chairman, so of course. . . ."

Agatha saw that Miss Neele wore stockings of silk and that her skirt was fashionably short.

"I hope my husband isn't overworking you," she said.

Miss Neele smiled nervously. "I told him I was overworked and he said, 'No, you're overweight. What you need is a week or two at a spa and a dose of those horrid-tasting waters.' So next Monday I'm off to the north."

She tidied some documents with unnecessary zeal. "Perhaps there isn't much point in waiting?"

"I've probably waited too long already," Agatha replied.

The secretary, who was somewhat embarrassed, turned her back in order to open a file cabinet, and began to search for something as if its discovery were urgent. Over her shoulder she said, "Would you like something to . . . ?"

But the Colonel's wife had already left.

Late that afternoon Agatha arrived back at Styles. She found Charlotte Fisher in the conservatory, which abutted on the dining room, taking bulbs from small pots and bedding them in larger bowls. She wore an apron and a concentrated frown.

Agatha stopped in the doorway. Miss Fisher glanced at her.

"It can't have been that bad."

"Where's Rosalind?" Agatha asked.

"On her way to bed. She wanted you to read to her."

"She wants Archie to read to her."

Agatha picked up a pot of poinsettias. "I do hate these, don't you? Can't think why we have them." She put the pot down. "He says he hates the garden, Charlotte. I think he doesn't like me paying for things. If we got rid of the house, lived somewhere smaller . . ."

Miss Fisher put down her trowel and asked with mild irony, "Somewhere with a golf course?"

"Yes," said Agatha enthusiastically.

"Come and have some tea," said Miss Fisher and led Agatha through the dining room and into the drawing room, where a fire burned in the grate. It was a comfortable, almost elegant room, a mixture of antiques with one or two contemporary lamps and cabinets. Damask curtains were drawn across the window alcove and an embroidered fringed shawl was draped over the grand piano. A tray bore a plate of neatly trimmed cucumber sandwiches and a pot of Earl Grey tea.

Agatha knelt down close to the fire beside her wire-haired terrier, who turned over on his back in pleasurable abandon.

She stared into the fire for a while, then turned to her secretary. "If only I'd got there in time."

"Were you late?"

"No, Charlotte. In time to see Mother before she died. I should have been there, you know."

"Stop brooding and drink your tea," said Charlotte Fisher. "You should start playing the piano again. Something to take your mind off things. Why not try one of those nice sauces you used to concoct?"

"You mean, why not start writing again," Agatha said. She went on stroking the dog. "Perhaps I should ask Campbell for help?"

"Don't bring it up tonight. After all, he is the Colonel's brother, and you'll only get upset."

Agatha turned to face her secretary. "I went to the office this afternoon. I saw her."

"Now that was daft," Miss Fisher said.

Chapter 2

Archibald Christie's mother, Mrs. Helmsley, had remarried after her first husband died, and had brought back to Dorking, a town a stone's throw from Sunningdale, the relics of her life in India. Ivory tusks, elephant feet, teak and mahogany cabinets, brass urns, Ghurka swords. Many sepia-tinted photographs of Colonial panoply crowded her drawing room, which was too small for its contents.

Mrs. Helmsley resented her reduced circumstances as much as she resented modern trends. She didn't like radio sets, central heating, cheeky servants, and the new rich. She especially disapproved of the new rich who had managed to infiltrate the Sunningdale Golf Club. She would say of them: "They just take up space and wear dreadful new shoes."

Mrs. Helmsley didn't really like her daughter-in-law, either. "She feels too much, that girl," said

Mrs. Helmsley. She didn't believe in nervous breakdowns, certainly not those that lasted six months. She disapproved of Agatha's demonstrative love for Archie, her demands upon her son, her recent hysterical outbursts when threatened with the loss of him. She thought her daughter-in-law disturbed, considered she needed to "buckle down to things and pull herself together." She sensed in Agatha unpredictable behavior: a woman who wrote so compulsively about murder was not acceptable.

That evening, when her daughter-in-law arrived to dine accompanied by Charlotte Fisher, Mrs. Helmsley welcomed them effusively. Agatha knew that her mother-in-law always exaggerated her expression of welcome when she felt most hostile. Mrs. Helmsley made sure that during dinner the conversation was confined to golf.

After dinner, while Charlotte Fisher read by the drawing-room fire, Agatha sat at the card table with her mother-in-law and Capt. Philip Rankin, an officer friend and contemporary of Archie's, known to his men as the "Weasel." Rankin's life fell into three compartments: disciplining his men, getting drunk with his equals, and "hosing" the ladies, as he put it. He considered Archie had made a poor choice of wife and, knowing relations were precarious between them, delighted in tormenting Agatha.

Mrs. Helmsley divided the tiles into four sets of thirty-six and began to build her wall in preparation for the play. Mah-jongg, a game almost out of fashion in the United States, where it had been revived, was popular in Sunningdale. Few people understood the obscure rules but they liked handling the ivory tiles painted with dragons, flowers, and seasonal emblems. Both Christie brothers were expected to join the play.

Agatha apologized for her husband's absence. "Archie'll be late," she said.

"Works himself to the bone." Rankin smiled.

"I can't see what's so virtuous about work," she answered as a diversion. "We never had to. Nor did my father. Never did a hand's turn and he was very agreeable."

"But *you* work, my dear," Rankin said, placing his tiles in two layers, face down.

"I make puzzles, I don't work."

"Wonder why you bother."

Agatha looked flustered. "Well, you can do it anywhere, in your own time. I used to make up stories as a child. I expect it's to do with my mother. She didn't believe in school. Thought it destroyed your brain."

"Waste of time for gels," said Rankin, consulting his watch. "Settle down and breed."

"I quite agree," Agatha said, enthusiastically. "Family life's the best there is. Much more fun than any other kind."

"There isn't any other kind," Mrs. Helmsley, absently.

The conversation came abruptly to an end when the telephone rang. An elderly maid came into the room. "The Colonel, ma'am," she said.

"For me?" Agatha asked.

The maid shook her head. "He said to tell his mother that he won't be able to come."

"He's been held up," Agatha mumbled.

"I expected so," said Mrs. Helmsley. "Campbell can take his place."

"I can't understand why he can't come," her daughter-in-law said.

"Keep him on a tight rein, don't you?" Rankin leered.

Agatha looked at him and wondered what it was she'd done to merit such hate. If ever she wrote anything again, Rankin would serve as model for the villain.

Campbell Christie's entrance brought some relief to this mirthless group. Younger than his brother, Archie, Campbell was a military instructor at the Royal Military Academy at Woolwich, an officer who commanded respect and affection. Agatha needed to believe that Campbell alone in an alien world might offer her help.

"Evening, Mother," he said while he kissed Agatha and shook hands with Philip Rankin. When he was comfortably settled, the game began.

"That fellow who threw himself at the train," Campbell said. "Just heard his wife left him."

"No," said Rankin. "It was money trouble."

"Money, was it?" snorted Campbell Christie. "Rule India, then find yourself breeding chickens."

Rankin roared with laughter. "Silly way to kill yourself. Should have blown out his brains."

"There!" Campbell declared, laying down his tiles. "I've got a Hand of Heaven—how about that?"

"Stationmaster had to sweep up the nuts and bolts," Rankin continued. "Blood all over the place. How are you going to kill yourself, Agatha?"

"Arsenic," she answered harshly. "You see, that's the most painful of all the poisons. You die very slowly. There's no antidote, no relief."

"Why not try it on somebody else? That's what you do in your books."

She jumped up from the table and ran out, closely followed by Charlotte Fisher and Mrs. Helmsley.

"I won't be mocked!" she cried. "Why didn't Campbell say something?"

"Well, my dear," said Mrs. Helmsley, "you shouldn't make such silly threats all the time."

"Archie's driven me—"

"It's nothing to do with my son, and I simply can't have your secretary calling every day saying you're going to kill yourself. It's very . . . unbecoming."

Agatha said "Please help me" in a way that might have melted the stoniest heart. But her mother-in-law told her to calm down, to remember she was a grown woman, and to go home. Thus humiliated and silenced, Agatha allowed Charlotte to lead her out.

On the journey back to Styles, Charlotte Fisher talked of the strictly inconsequential. "He was driving too fast," she said as she opened the door of the house. "Knocked down four ladies at the golf course. No one felt they could reprimand the Prince of Wales for that kind of thing, so they're building a special wall."

Agatha, who was not listening, took off her cloak.

"He's not home," she said. She began to climb the stairway.

Miss Fisher said, "Now try to sleep."

Agatha put on satin pajamas and brushed her hair. Then she lay on her bed and planned how she would order her life and regain her happiness. But in sleep the will failed her. She dreamed that she was eleven years old. It was the year her father died, the year her red hair reached her waist. She entered the hall of the family house in Devon. There, in an expectant line, was Archie in full uniform. Beside him her mother, her grandmother, all the family servants, and many unsmiling officials, dressed as if for a funeral.

"We've been waiting for you, darling," her mother said. "You didn't come home."

"But I didn't know, Mother," she said, all the time staring at Archibald Christie like a rabbit fixed by a stoat.

"What do you want of me?" she asked him.

And he replied, "To cut out your heart. That's what's required."

She woke from the dream, sweating with fear, and saw in the dim morning light that the other side of the sheet was still folded neatly back. An hour later she heard her husband's car turn into the drive of the house. She sat up, shaking with sick relief. She eventually put on a dressing gown, washed her pale face in cold water, and combed her hair at the dressing table. Then she went down the stairs and into the dining room.

Bright sunlight flooded the cream-paneled room. At the head of the polished table sat Archibald Christie, bathed and laundered, eating his break-

fast while he read the morning newspaper. A
Georgian silver coffeepot gleamed in front of
him.

Agatha helped herself to breakfast from the
sideboard and sat down next to her husband.
The sun hit Christie's blue eyes as he said good
morning to his wife; it streaked off the silver,
glowed on the polished wood, and warmed Agatha's
back. There was nothing she would not have done
to keep this world together. She spoke up with
manic willfulness.

"I've decided I'm not going to mind about your
weekend, Archie. Nobody will ever know, and I'll
go to Beverley. I'll take lots of books and drive,
which will take hours. When I get back it will be
as if your weekend never happened."

"And next weekend?"

"Please, not next weekend."

"But you agreed," he said testily. "I can't let
Nancy down. I've given her my word."

"Your word! You're betraying us."

Her husband stretched out his hand to take
hers. "You can't betray what you're no longer
loyal to," he said gently. "Does that make sense?
I do love you, but we've been together . . . a very
long time. Anyway, I have a very low opinion
of myself."

"I have the highest opinion of you," Agatha
said.

"No, you don't."

"No, I don't." She smiled. "But I do love you
enormously."

Her husband was not won over. "I just don't

want to be your ever-loving husband, and I won't be part of your scheme."

"I'll leave!" she cried. "I'll go away."

"We go away every day, every time we leave a room," he said briskly. "Look, you confront me. Then, when I tell you the truth, you won't face it." He poured himself another cup of coffee, drew in his darting anger: he needed his wife's cooperation.

"Agatha, I really want a divorce."

"No, darling, you don't. You wanted one after Mother died, because I was so unpleasant to be with. But I'm better now. We'll have grand times. Go to Africa again."

"I don't want to go to Africa," he said. "Not with you. You're doing very well. It can be done without . . . embarrassment. A lawyer will find a woman you can name."

"There is a woman," Agatha said.

"You can't name her. I love her and I want to marry her. Decently."

"But I shall name her."

Archie Christie exploded. "You'd name her, all right. You'd go to any lengths. I tell you, Agatha, you've become unbalanced and destructive."

She stood up to put her arms around her husband, to stop his words. He pushed her aside, so that she fell to her knees. At that moment, Jane, the parlormaid, came into the room carrying a pot of fresh coffee.

"Get up," Archie said under his breath. Agatha stood up awkwardly while the maid, who had registered the domestic row, beat her retreat. Christie looked at his wife with hatred.

"You particularly play up in front of the servants."

"That's not true," she said quietly, all her endeavor collapsed.

"You dramatize everything. But your tactics are poor," he went on. "I suggest you stop following me to the office. You've no sense of dignity." He looked her in the eye. "If I gave you enough rope, you'd probably hang yourself."

"Let's stop," she begged. "Let's find a way."

He got up. "I'm not with you any more. Not now nor ever again."

Agatha heard her husband address a servant outside in the hall. "Make no arrangements for me," he said. Then she heard him shut the front door behind him. His wife sat very still for some time. She had the same fixed and terrified look of the child in her dream.

At midday Charlotte Fisher found her mistress still in a dressing gown and lying on her bed. "I called that Miss Neele for you. Said you needed copies of the household bills."

"Did she say where she was going?"

"She told me about the holiday before I had a chance to worm it out of her."

"Which spa is it, Charlotte?"

"She said she was going to Harrogate. I told her I knew it well, and which hotel was she staying at. It's the Valencia. Two weeks. Now I think you should put it all out of your mind."

Agatha covered her head with her arm.

"Wouldn't you know Archie'd choose somewhere like that. Discreetly out of season. Full of old people. Nobody'd see him there. I wish I were dead."

Miss Fisher sat on the bed and stroked her mistress's hair. "I'd better stay, hadn't I? You don't look well."

"No, Charlotte dear," she reassured her. "You go off. I'm all right and I'll see you later."

By mid-afternoon Agatha had managed to dress. She put her dog, Peter, into the car. She picked up her daughter from school. She was relieved that child and dog kept each other entertained. On the spur of the moment she decided to drive to her mother-in-law's and, once arrived, sat among Mrs. Helmsley's relics perfectly still, gazing into space, once or twice laughed loudly for no apparent reason, kissed and hugged her daughter. Her mother-in-law thought she seemed improved.

Capt. Philip Rankin's mock Tudor cottage was some twenty miles from Styles. It was conveniently situated between his army base and his golf course. In one of the bedrooms, on the night of December third, Nancy Neele was changing for dinner. She wore camiknickers over a suspender belt, stockings, and shoes. She sat before the looking glass penciling her eyebrows. She applied lipstick carefully so as not to exaggerate the shape of her lips. She hummed to herself. Archie Christie knocked at the door and entered before she had time to find her wrap. He was already changed for dinner. He looked at Nancy with shy delight. "You don't mind?"

Nancy smiled at him through the mirror. "Philip might mind," she said.

"No worry. Commissioned together. Known me forever. Adores you."

Nancy began to powder her nose. To Archie she promised a bland, a more supple life. He moved behind her and gently slid the straps off her shoulders. Nancy swiveled her legs about to face him.

"Stand up," he said. She stood up slowly. "Take it right off." Nancy turned her back on him, pushed the camiknickers down, and looked over her shoulder.

"You're most frightfully pretty," Archie said.

"And obedient."

"We'd better go downstairs," he said. He was a prudent man.

When the housekeeper, Mrs. Stocks, had served dinner, Philip Rankin asked for brandy and cigars and went on with his story. He leaned close to Nancy, his mustcline face shining with the heat of the room. "Well, Archie told me it was a fancy-dress ball. Had myself kitted out in a penguin's suit and showed up at Warwick. The butler laid out the suit *and* the flippers. Never turned a hair."

Mrs. Stocks filled the three glasses once more. Rankin lifted his. "Here's to your future," he said. "Hope you'll both be very happy. You deserve it." Archie and Nancy smiled their thanks. Rankin drew on his cigar. "Open the window, would you, Mrs. Stocks," he said. The housekeeper pulled back the curtains and opened the latticed window wide.

"Do go on," Nancy said.

"So I went down for cocktails," Rankin continued, "in my full penguin regalia, and everyone else was in white tie and tails. You devil, Archie!"

The laughter from the room blew out into the sharp night, where Agatha stood a few yards from the window. She saw her husband rise and kiss Nancy Neele on the lips. Then she turned and ran to her car.

In desperation, her brain raced to an orderly solution.

When she got back to Styles, Agatha went straight to her study and wrote three letters. She placed one to Charlotte Fisher and another to her husband on the table in the hall. The third letter, addressed to her brother-in-law, she put into her handbag. She climbed to her bedroom and began to shove clothes—a skirt, an evening dress, several pairs of shoes, randomly chosen—into a hand valise. Into her handbag she stuffed some twenty-pound bank notes, which she took from a drawer. She put on a fur coat and picked up the case. She opened the door to her daughter's bedroom, where a small night lamp lit the sleeping child. She kissed Rosalind tenderly and crept out of the room.

"I'll let you know where I am tomorrow morning," she told the housemaid, who noticed that part of a silk dress hung out of the poorly packed valise.

Agatha climbed into her car and sat at the wheel. The lantern over the entrance of the house dimly lit her knuckled fist pressed into her mouth. Eventually, she drove off wildly and at speed in the direction of Newlands Corner.

Chapter 3

It was just after eight on the morning of December fourth, the light still dim and the earth hard frozen. Over the brow of a hill, at the point where the Guildford/Dorking road descends into a wooded valley toward the Pilgrims Way, a poorly dressed countrywoman dragged a small dogcart. Beside her walked a grave-looking child, no more than six years old. The only habitation at Newlands Corner was a one-story café at the crest of the hill. As the countrywoman approached the café, she noticed that on the opposite side of the road, some one hundred yards down the hill, a two-seater car was nosed at a precarious angle into a thicket. She set down her cart, directed her boy to stand by it, and walked toward the car. A figure appeared to be slumped over the wheel, and the vehicle was covered in frost.

The woman opened the car door. The fur coat that embraced the steering wheel fell back on the seat.

She felt momentarily startled, the victim of some weird trick. Swiftly, she began to search the car, discarded a stubby umbrella, two pairs of women's shoes, one of them muddied, a cardigan jumper, and a skirt. Inside a hand valise she dug out an evening dress and a driving license. The woman threw down the license and continued her search.

As she backed out of the car, a firm hand grabbed her, spun her around.

"What do you think you're doing!" shouted the proprietor of the café on the hill.

The woman startled. "I thought there was somebody in the car."

"You thought to help yourself," said Mr. Luland, already searching in the car. He picked up the driver's license. It read, "Mrs. Agatha Mary Clarissa Christie." Luland shook his head. He looked at the woman standing sullenly alongside the car, focused his fear and suspicion on her, took her by the arm, and dragged her up the hill.

Luland's café was a shabby place built of plaster and wood slats. The owner, who had some dim sense of the bleakness of his life, had pinned photographs of bright racing cars to the walls. He told the countrywoman and her child to wait for the police. Then he finished his breakfast.

"It was about eight, I believe," Luland told Police Constable Reynolds from the local station. "Lights must have been left on because the battery'd gone dead. Car's not damaged. But how did it get down that slope? Either it slid down off the road, or somebody drove it down. Could have been killed. But there's no sign of struggle, no blood." He offered the young policeman a cup of tea. "Now, what kind of woman would leave a valuable coat like that in this weather? Doesn't make sense," he added. "Think she was alone?"

Police Constable Reynolds inspected the driver's license. Then he telephoned Deputy Chief Constable Kenward of the Surrey police. Reynolds took the countrywoman's name, gave her child a coin, and went to inspect the contents of the car. The grassy slope down which the vehicle had plunged was now partly unfrozen. Sunlight glinted off the melting frost, and a herd of cows ambled along the track adjacent to the deserted car, which looked, at this friendly hour, disturbingly out of place.

Meanwhile, Superintendent Kenward telephoned Styles. He asked for the Colonel and, when told he was not at home, informed Charlotte Fisher that Mrs. Christie's car had been discovered, empty.

He said that the evidence pointed either to an accident or to foul play. He asked Charlotte Fisher whether the Colonel had been with Mrs. Christie on the previous evening. The girl was terribly distraught.

"The Colonel's away for the weekend, Superintendent."

"Away where, may I ask?"

"Staying with friends, sir. A Captain Rankin, at Dorking."

"I suggest you contact Colonel Christie and tell him I wish to speak to him. Have you any idea where Mrs. Christie might be?"

"No, I haven't. She left home last night saying she would let us know where she was in the morning. She hasn't been well, Superintendent. Anything might have happened. I'm her secretary, Charlotte Fisher. I was out last night when Mrs. Christie left the house. She told the housemaid she would contact us in the morning."

"You have no idea what might have happened?"

Charlotte Fisher paused and then she said, "Mrs. Christie left letters, one for her husband and one for me. Mine was the letter of a very distraught person. Her mother died recently and Mrs. Christie suffered a nervous breakdown. This weekend she had made plans to go to Beverley, in Yorkshire. But in her letter she asked me to cancel the arrangement."

"She was intending to go alone, without her husband?"

"Yes, sir. That's correct."

"We've received reports in the last few months that Mrs. Christie has threatened to kill herself. Can you tell me anything about those threats?"

"I know nothing about them at all, Superintendent."

"Thank you, Miss Fisher. I'll be in touch with you later in the morning."

Less than an hour later William Kenward stepped out of his Armstrong Siddeley at the brow of the hill at Newland's Lane. He was a tall, burly, dutiful police officer, conscientious and reliable. In his spare time he liked to feed pigeons and out-of-work ex-prisoners. Kenward was a Christian and his subordinates knew his bark was worse than his bite.

"Find anything?" he asked Reynolds.

The young policeman held up a green velour hat.

"Found this," he said, "fifty feet away, and a bit of cloth. Found them just over there. No footprints, sir. Nothing. The ground was so frozen this morning. Couldn't trace the tire marks. Think it was an accident or deliberate? Of course," the young constable continued, "there's the possibility the lady was kidnapped."

Kenward lit up his pipe reflectively. He had his own theory.

Archibald Christie, warned by Miss Fisher, was on his way home from Rankin's cottage. He read his wife's letter.

"Christ, how indulgent," he said to the secretary. Then he looked at the letter again. "She says she had to get away. Get away where?"

"In her letter to me she asked me to cancel Beverley," Miss Fisher said, "so she's not gone to Yorkshire."

"Bloody inconsiderate," said the Colonel. "The scandal. What on earth did you tell that officer?"

"I told him she'd recently had a nervous breakdown because of her mother. I told him she'd left letters."

"That was incredibly foolish of you."

Miss Fisher looked stubborn. "He told me he'd received reports that Agatha'd threatened to take her life."

Archie Christie lost his temper. "I suppose you were responsible?"

"I've nothing to do with rumors of any kind. But that officer thinks your wife is dead."

"Dead, that's absurd. I must warn my mother."

Miss Fisher said quietly, "She may be dead."

She held out her letter. "This is from a suicidal woman."

"Nonsense." The Colonel brandished his own letter. "This is full of lively threats—dangerous threats, Charlotte. Or novelists' stuff. Probably intends to put it all into some wretched book. Well, I won't be used." He glanced once more at his letter, crumpled it, and threw it on the fire. "What else was in your letter, Charlotte?"

The girl said nothing.

"Well, I suggest you burn your letter, too."

"No, Colonel," said Miss Fisher, "I'm not going to do that."

Kenward's office was spartan. It contained filing cabinets, one overhead lamp with a green shade, a tray of bird seed, a bulletin board, and two oak desks. At one of which, on this morning of December fourth, sat Kenward's secretary-cum-assistant, Miss Jennifer Grummit, an amiable, pear-shaped spinster, much in love with the upper class. She was happily buried in the Christmas issue of the fashionable magazine *The Sketch* when John Foster, of the *Sunningdale Echo,* poked his head around the door. Kenward took advantage of local reporters, as was the custom in the police force at that time. He called Foster in to get information out of suspects or to break alibis, the kind of work he felt was too sleazy or too improper for his own men.

Miss Grummit acknowledged John's arrival by reading aloud a passage from *The Sketch* of particular fascination: " 'The Maharajah of Alwar wore a most exciting headdress with many horns laced together with gold.' Now why would the Duke and Duchess of York entertain a savage with horns?" She looked up for John's reaction.

"Horns is nothing, Grummit. Horns is under-dressed in India. Now, what's he want me for? Anything juicy?"

Miss Grummit tore herself unwillingly from the social calendar to carry out her duty. "When did we get those rumors about Mrs. Christie threatening to take her life?"

Foster looked interested. "A month ago. Gone and done it, has she?"

Miss Grummit shrugged. "Or disappeared. The Superintendent thinks you could help him. Wants you to talk to the servants."

"That's right," said Kenward as he marched into his office, followed by Police Constable Reynolds. "Now take down this description, Grummit! Missing from her home, the Styles, Sunningdale, Berkshire, Mrs. Agatha Mary Clarissa Christie; height five feet seven inches . . ." He stopped in front of his secretary. "You shouldn't read that rubbish." Miss Grummit put *The Sketch* away in a drawer. "Hair red"—he consulted his notes—"shingled, part grey, complexion fair, build slight; dressed in grey stockinet skirt, green jumper, grey and dark grey cardigan and small velour hat; wearing a platinum ring with one pearl; no wedding ring; black handbag with purse containing perhaps five or ten pounds."

Kenward drew breath. "Phone it through local and London."

Foster offered his services. "Want me to ferret this one out?" Kenward, who had opened the window and was scattering grain on the sill for the benefit of three overfed pigeons, took his time replying. He objected to police complicity with the press, but he knew it produced results.

"Keep away from the house," he said.

"If I get my story into the bargain," John Foster answered.

Wally Stanton was in his special cubicle separated from the *Globe-Enquirer*'s newsroom when Foster's telephone call came through. Wally had been wondering how to fill his column. He looked at his notes, then made out four categories. Under "Human Interest," he wrote: "Casualty of the General Strike. Welsh Miner's family dies of starvation." He looked at the details. Nothing new there. He tried another story, about a woman who had just come out of hiding. "Seven months after the General Strike Mrs. Georgina Butt, a rich Gloucestershire widow, has returned to the land of the living. On the first day of the strike last May, Mrs. Butt fled, in the company of a Great Dane, to a nearby cave. She took with her a large supply of smoked meat and tinned biscuit. She was discovered last week by a farmer, Mr. John Sprigg, who was able to persuade Mrs. Butt that the Bolshie threat had been averted, that Englishmen were sleeping safely in their beds, and that God was still in his Heaven."

Wally was not enamored of the story. The starving miner's family would have gone down better in America. He could have made his fellow countrymen weep with that kind of stuff. But in England he couldn't pull at their heartstrings so easily. You had to be subtle to make any kind of social comment.

"Be vigilant," his old editor on the *Denver Post* used to say. "Tell your story straight and true and you will help to make a better world." Wally, as he approached middle age, no longer told stories straight and true. Under a section titled "Overheards," he noted that Lady Cunard had found Lady Sackville sitting up in bed eating *pâté de foie gras* with a shoehorn. Next, he counseled socially aspiring Americans in England to travel with their own linen and sauce cooks. He reported that the well-known novelist Scott Fitzgerald had given a Negro lift boy a bottle of deodorant for Christmas.

He picked up a chrome-backed blotting pad, turned it over, and stared at his own reflection. The neat, elegant face read reproach and disappointment. He rearranged it, as he did in public, so that his look said: "I'm at a party and I'm pleased to be alive."

His secretary, Polly, who was twenty-four and no fool, stood watching her boss from the door.

"I like what you see." She laughed.

"Tell you something, Polly," he said. "There's one very good thing about this country. They don't promise you too much. In Loveland, Colorado, they tell you you're going to inherit the earth. When my brother found out that wasn't the case, he killed himself." Wally smiled to cover his own portentousness.

Polly said, "There's a John Foster on the line. Says he met you last week at some lunch."

Wally picked up the telephone. "Hello, John.

How you doin'? . . . Yes, all the time in the world . . .

"It's a good story, John. Why don't you use it yourself? . . . Hm. That's very decent of you. Sure we can share it, only you'll have to accept a fee."

Wally put his hand over the receiver. "Would you mind sitting on my knee?" he said to Polly.

Polly tucked herself into her employer's left arm. "Shall I take notes?"

"Yes. Write down 'The Silent Pool.'" He rolled his eyes dramatically.

"Story of the century, John," he said, and yawned for Polly's benefit. "Good of you to let me know." He put down the receiver and kissed Polly.

"What was all that about?" she asked.

He pushed her gently off his knee.

"Think I'll give the swank crowd a break. I'm taking up crime."

By 3:00 P.M. on Saturday afternoon half a dozen reporters, a group of local people well wrapped against the cold, and a number of police had gathered at the Silent Pool at the foot of the North Downs, a mile or so below Newlands Corner, where Agatha Christie's car had been found.

Deputy Chief Constable Kenward was in charge of an operation to dredge the clear pool. Five or six men on opposite banks were dragging a long rope through the water. Attached to the rope were four curled spikes like giant fishhooks.

Among the onlookers was John Foster and, beside him, Wally Stanton, who wore a tweed coat and jaunty cap. He had positioned himself on a shooting stick.

Kenward was trying to supervise the search for the body of the missing novelist and at the same time answer questions from the press.

"She drove away from her home at nine forty-five last night," he said. "She left a letter for her secretary telling her to cancel a trip to Beverley, in Yorkshire."

"We heard Mrs. Christie had been sighted early this morning," said one of the reporters.

"Several witnesses have come forward," Kenward replied. "A porter at Milford Station, about five miles from Guildford, told us that at seven A.M., when he opened the station, a woman approached him and asked the time of the next train to Portsmouth. He said she wore a mackintosh and that her hair was covered with frost. Now, a more convincing witness is Ernest Cross, a farmhand. An hour ago he told us that just after six this morning a hatless woman stopped him at Newlands Corner, moaning and holding her hands to her head. He helped her start her car and she drove away toward Guildford. Trouble is, the car didn't match Mrs. Christie's."

"I bet she's disguised as a man," said a wag from the *News of the World*, "and hiding out in London."

"Come on," said another reporter, "what's the truth, Superintendent? You're not out here in the bleedin' cold dragging that pool to catch—"

"Pollywogs?" Wally suggested. "Sorry. 'Tiddlers,' I believe you call them."

The group laughed, Kenward looked offended,

and John Foster showed solidarity with his star guest by adding, "We should have brought our jam jars."

"We've traipsed across the terrain this morning," Kenward went on, "Petersfield to Dorking, Godalming to Reigate."

"Looking for a corpse?" somebody asked.

"Yes, that's correct."

"Think somebody did her in?" someone else asked.

"*Daily News,* sir. What makes you so sure Mrs. Christie's dead?"

"I can't talk to you now," he said and turned back to his men. "Into the boats now. We'll pull the rope across once more. This time not so fast."

Wally said to John Foster, "You're sure about those suicide threats?" John nodded. "And you're telling me she specified this pool?"

Wally was thinking of making his way back to London and the "swank crowd" when three men led by Police Constable Reynolds arrived on the scene and walked up to Kenward. They were Archie Christie, his brother, Campbell, and Philip Rankin.

"Good morning, sir," said Kenward. "Were you able to identify the car?"

"It belongs to my wife," said the Colonel, tersely.

"When did you last see your wife?"

"I last saw her at a quarter past nine yesterday morning."

Kenward drew Archie and his party away from the reporters.

"Did she seem distressed in any way?" he continued.

"She was well in view of the state of her health."

"Miss Fisher told me on the telephone that Mrs. Christie was suffering from depression."

"That's correct. Her mother died recently."

"Well, sir, we've received rumors about your wife, that she threatened to kill herself."

The Colonel folded his arms. "I'd hardly think you'd deal in rumors. From whom?"

"I can't reveal that. They were lodged at my station."

Wally Stanton moved his shooting stick nearer to the action.

"I know nothing about rumors," Archie continued. "I left home early yesterday morning for a weekend with Captain Rankin." He indicated Rankin, who regarded the policeman haughtily. "It's a common practice of mine. My wife knew my whereabouts. The first I heard of her disappearance was this morning."

"Excuse me, sir, but have you any witness to your whereabouts last night?"

"I believe I just told you, Superintendent, that I spent the night with Captain Rankin."

"Might you for any reason have left during the course of the night? Your wife, you say, knew your whereabouts. Did she by any chance try and contact you at Captain Rankin's?"

"She did not."

"What time did you retire, sir?"

"I suppose about midnight."

"So you could possibly have left Captain Rankin's house during the early hours of the morning?"

"I did not leave Captain Rankin's house till this morning."

"And you have a witness?"

Christie glanced toward Rankin. "Of course I have no witness. I wouldn't consider wandering around the country in the middle of the night—"

"Unless your wife had been in touch with you."

"My wife did *not* get in touch with me. Now, have you any further questions? You must realize I'm extremely upset and the sooner—"

Kenward interrupted. "I gather from Miss Fisher that your wife left letters."

"Yes. Letters of a very nervous woman. She wrote to me that she was going away for the weekend, and that she felt rather queer. Her letter referred to a purely personal matter and has no bearing whatsoever on her disappearance."

"We may need to see that letter, Colonel."

"I'm afraid I burnt it. This is my brother," he added, as if to change the subject.

"Good afternoon, sir." Kenward returned to his interrogation. "You have no idea where your wife could be?"

"No, and I'm quite sure she'll not return till all is quiet. Therefore, I strongly urge you to keep the matter"—he looked over his shoulder, noticed how close Wally was, and lowered his voice— "private."

Kenward said stubbornly, "Your wife may be dead. It's my duty to do all I can."

"Dead!" said the Colonel. "Rubbish!"

"Does your wife own a green hat?"

"Most probably. I'd say that was rather a foolish question. Anything else?"

"Not now."

"Well, you may count on my co-operation," Archie said and, with his two cohorts, he turned to leave.

John Foster crept up to Wally's side. "What'd he say?"

"It's what he didn't say that's interesting," Wally answered. "What do you know about him, John?"

"Won a lot of medals in the war. Drove a train last spring in the strike."

The men pulling the rope across the water had now met. From one of the spikes a policeman retrieved a woman's shoe and presented it to Kenward. People rushed forward to see what had been found.

"Oldest damn shoe I ever saw," Wally said and, with John lumbering along at his side, he moved off along the edge of the Silent Pool toward the main road. "Now why is your superintendent so sure Mrs. Christie's in that pool? A suicide threat's one thing but . . ."

"Somebody told him Mrs. Christie'd drowned a character in one of her books here, but there's something more to it. Got something up his sleeve, old Bill. Thinks she's been done in, I suspect."

"I thought you and he were joined at the hip."

John looked doleful. "I do his dirty work, and he feeds me the odd bone. 'Fraid I've wasted your time."

They continued along the bank. John said, "King John chased a naked maiden into that pool."

It was the only bit of information he had to offer. "She just kept walking in till she drowned."

Wally laughed. "Heard of Aimee Semple McPherson?" John shook his thatched head. "Lady Evangelist. Walked into the Pacific some months ago. Stayed there thirty-seven days before Jesus intervened. She said, "If I hope and pray, will you do the rest?' And Jesus said, 'Of course I will.' Turned out Aimee was having a tumble with a fellow the whole time. Now, where's Mrs. Christie?

"There's a parlormaid, may know something. Well, let's find her."

It took this oddly matched couple of sleuths three hours to hunt down Jane Miller. Since Styles was already surrounded by a cordon of police, the place could not be approached. But a telephone call to the house, which was answered by a servant, revealed that the girl was off duty for the afternoon.

The clergyman's wife, who knew everybody in the village, was tried, but she had gone to Dorking for a leprosy-relief bazaar. Wally wanted to go. "I'm not going to miss out on a leper party," he said. He was, however, dissuaded by John Foster, who felt for the first time in his life that he had the bit between his teeth.

"Postmaster knows the girl," he said. "We'd better stop off there."

Postmaster Dodds, who had an unfocused left eye, was measuring out boiled sweets for a small boy. Mr. Dodds also stocked skeins of wool and knitting patterns and tins of sardines, most of which had gathered dust because of his slow turnover. The postmaster was halfway through writing a book called "Sunningdale, Then and Now," and his heart was in history rather than commerce.

John Foster introduced his famous colleague.

"You know Mrs. Christie?" Wally asked.

"Comes in here most days."

"What's she like?"

"Mrs. Christie? She's a very charming lady. Very brainy."

"A bit unstable, you think?"

Dodds's bad eye veered farther sideways. "Good gracious no, Mr. Stanton. She's not been well these past months but she's not wrong in the head."

Foster said, "I've a message for that Jane Miller. Works at Styles. Now where would we find her?"

"Village hall, I expect," said Dodds. "She always goes dancing on a Saturday."

The Saturday night dance at the Sunningdale Church Hall was a small and desultory affair. There were no more than two dozen young people attending, most of them domestic servants with nowhere else to go on their half-day of leisure. A brass band played, and at the side of the room a number of young girls sat hoping to be asked to dance. One of them was Jane, the small, fresh-faced parlormaid from Styles.

"There she is," John pointed her out triumphantly. "Evening, Jane." He grinned at the girl.

"Evening, John," said Jane, her eyes fixed on Wally Stanton.

The girl on Jane's left politely moved over a seat, allowing the two men to take a chair on each side of their quarry.

"Your Colonel's in a bit of a spot," John opened, undiplomatically. "Think she's dead?"

Jane's little pinched face collapsed. "She's a lovely lady."

"Care to dance?" Wally asked.

"Oooh yes, I would," she answered and took Wally's arm.

They began to waltz to a mournful tune. Wally smiled and Jane smiled readily back.

"You're a friend of John's?" she asked unbelievingly.

"As a matter of fact, I'm Mrs. Christie's American publisher. Mr. Foster here has been interviewing me."

"Oh, that explains it," she said.

"You waltz very well, Miss Miller."

"Especially as I don't get asked much."

"Well," Wally said, "you look pretty cheerful about it."

"It's what's in yourself that makes you happy."

Her partner nodded sagely. "Or unhappy," he added. "Did Mrs. Christie mind a lot about her mother?"

"Well, yes," said the parlormaid. "But that's . . ."

Wally's eyes invited confidence.

"To tell you the truth," she went on, "that's not what it's all about."

"So, what do you think it's all about?"

"She had a rotten time."

"Think Mrs. Christie's done something?"

Jane said, "She was in a terrible way."

As the waltz ended, the band struck up a military two-step. Wally said he wasn't familiar with the dance, and led his partner back to her chair.

"Did you come here just to see me?" she asked.

"Yes, we did. I want to know what happened to Mrs. Christie."

The girl sighed. "Well, thanks for the dance all the same."

When the two men had left, Jane rejoined the line of working girls.

Outside, Wally said to John, "Your parlormaid wasn't much help."

Foster grinned. "But her friend was. Said the Colonel's off with his secretary. Threatened to leave his wife."

Chapter 4

Agatha Christie sat in the carriage of the train, staring ahead of her. Her hands were folded on her lap over a newspaper neatly creased to turn up a crossword puzzle. She wore a cloth coat, her stockings and shoes were noticeably muddied, and she traveled without luggage other than a hand valise. Neither the coat nor the valise was the same with which she had left Styles on the previous night.

It was just after 6:00 P.M. as the train drew into the station of the Yorkshire spa at Harrogate. Agatha made her way along the platform to the station exit. A sleety snow fell on the waiting taxicabs. Two brightly painted horse-drawn buses stood out in the dim light. They bore the liveries of the Grand Hotel and the Harrogate Hydro. Agatha stepped into the Hydro bus, sat back in the dark, closed her eyes, let her mouth droop open in an expression of pain that she had not allowed herself to show in a more public place.

The hotel at which the bus deposited its three passengers was an impressive Victorian building of grey Yorkshire stone. Agatha walked into the main lobby. The receptionist, an elderly man with a blond moustache who had seen spa visitors come and go, knew who was who, had once bowed to the Empress Marie of Russia, regarded Agatha with ill-concealed curiosity.

"I should like a room," she said.

"For how long, madam?" asked the receptionist.

"About a fortnight, I believe. How much do you charge?"

The man looked at his book. "We have a room at five guineas a week. There are others at five and a half guineas which overlook the garden."

"I'll take one overlooking the garden," Agatha said.

She was asked to sign, and the registry was placed before her. Agatha wrote: "Mrs. Teresa Neele." She paused momentarily. Then she added: "Cape Town, South Africa."

"Your luggage, madam?" the porter inquired.

"Just the hand valise," she said. "My luggage . . . My luggage has been lost."

Alone in her room Agatha removed her coat, washed her hands, and unpacked her small case. She took out a hot-water bottle, a comb, and two bottles with medical labels, one of which was marked "Poison." On the bedside table she stood up a leather-framed photograph of her child. Then, with no more to unpack, she sat on the edge of the single bed as if she had momentarily forgotten her next move.

Sometime later, still wearing the grey skirt and wool jumper and the muddied stockings in which she had arrived, Agatha entered the dining room of the Hydro. No more than four tables were occupied in the huge Edwardian room with its frieze of colored glass and ornately carved ceiling. There were several elderly guests, and one woman around thirty who was dining alone. She was pretty, with dark hair and a bright red mouth, and her expression conveyed candor and intelligence. Agatha, who sat nearby, noticed that she wore an inexpensive blouse and that the waiter addressed her as Miss Crawley, which suggested that her stay had been long or that she was a frequent visitor.

The same waiter presented Agatha with the menu. She scanned the printed card. "You make your own *pâté?*"

The man looked mildly affronted. "I'm not absolutely sure, madam."

She smiled. "Well, if you're not absolutely sure, I think we'll give it a miss. How about the hare soup?"

"Excellent, madam," said the elderly waiter.

"Then the *rognon de veau,*" she continued.

"You don't care for the fish?"

"No, not the fish, nor the pudding *diplomatique.*" She returned the menu. "Do you serve alcohol?"

"No, madam. Certainly not. We're a health spa, you realize," said the waiter, pleased to refuse so demanding a guest.

"I thought as much." Agatha smiled in return.

"I don't drink, as a matter of fact. Don't like the taste."

The waiter's injured look was recorded by Evelyn Crawley, who smiled collusively at her neighbor as she left the room. Agatha noticed that she walked with a stick.

It was the custom of the hotel to serve coffee in the Red Drawing Room, but by the time Agatha arrived, there was only one elderly man asleep in the corner of the room, and the young woman, Miss Crawley, at a table on her own. Agatha sat down at a friendly distance, neither too far nor too near, from the other woman. She picked up a copy of the *Harrogate Herald* and studied the published list of guests at present in town. The old man in the corner snored loudly.

Agatha caught her neighbor's eye and smiled.

"Why doesn't he go to bed and snore?" said the other woman.

Agatha nodded her agreement and sipped her coffee.

"I'm Evelyn Crawley."

"How do you do? I'm Mrs. Neele, Teresa." Agatha paused. "Is this your first time here?"

"Oh, no. I'm almost a regular."

"You come for hot baths?"

"More for special treatment. I've a bad back. I'm on my feet all day at work, which doesn't help. There's a therapist here does wonders." Evelyn Crawley had a lilting north-country accent.

Agatha said, "I've a bad back, too."

"Well, you couldn't choose a better place for treatment. Though it's not a barrel of laughs," she added.

Agatha smiled. "Did it used to be a . . . barrel of laughs?"

"The grand people used to come up from London in the summer. Kings and queens. Pavlova and Bernhardt entertained them. I used to hear all about it from my parents."

"They were regulars, too?"

"Oh, no. My father was headwaiter at this hotel and my mother worked at the baths. That's why I get special terms for treatment. I'm not the sort that belongs here." She laughed. "I'm afraid I'm boring you."

"Not at all," Agatha said. "What kind of people come at this time of year?"

"Let me see. Old people, like that old snorer. The halt and the maimed. And a few drunks. Where are you from, Mrs. Neele?"

"South Africa" came the reply.

"South Africa!"

Agatha nodded nervously. "Do forgive me, but I think I must be going," she said, and got up to leave.

She walked along a corridor to the hotel telephone booth, shut herself in, and asked the operator to get her the Valencia Hotel. "Has a Miss Nancy Neele arrived yet?" she asked. She held on for the answer. "Not until Monday? Could you check?" Agatha waited for the answer. "Thank you, no. There's no message."

The following day, Sunday, reduced the spa to a sepulchral quiet. A grey sky hung over the handsome Victorian town, and a cruel frost kept most guests indoors. Agatha was the exception.

She attended the service at St. Wilfred's, having requested the porter to recommend a High Church service. She explored the streets on foot, looked into the antique shops, made note of a papier-mâché table she wished to acquire, and listened to an afternoon recital of the music of Elgar and Bach, composers she particularly enjoyed.

She was not released from pain, but from inaction. With the ability to act, to make choices and decisions, she began to breathe freely again.

She spent the evening studying a book called *Hydrotherapy in Britain,* which she had taken from the hotel library. She read it in the privacy of her room, since the condition of her clothes had begun to attract embarrassing attention. She bathed, she washed her hair and rubbed it dry, combed it through. She climbed naked into the linen sheets, her muddied clothes laid out as if by a schoolgirl for a planned morrow.

Agatha picked up the first edition of Monday's *Daily Mail.* Halfway down the front page was a story about her disappearance. The article stated that the circumstances of the author's discovery were mysterious. Agatha's reaction was of surprise rather than fear; she had not calculated on the outside world's intrusion. With relief she noticed that the small photograph of herself was unrecognizable.

She paid for the newspaper, hurried out of the hotel, and walked rapidly down the hill in the direction of the bow-fronted shops.

She felt the sun on her skin and the sharp air in

her lungs. Even the newspaper article seemed a distant threat to her new reality, which was self-created and insulated from the world she had deserted. She knew what had to be done.

In the meantime, she could begin to take on a life she had for so long refused. She made many purchases. She bought several pairs of shoes, a pretty pincushion, some writing utensils, a powder box, rouge and lipstick, which she was not in the habit of wearing. Then she went into an elegant dress shop called Macdonald's, drawn there by a window display of a crêpe de Chine pajama suit and a Georgette evening gown with crystal beads. The shop, for Harrogate, was conspicuously fashionable. Inside, on long counters, were laid out the prettiest garments. The manager, a woman with crimped hair and an affected accent, busied happily over Agatha. She fetched her a snakeskin bag, some lingerie of crêpe de soie, silk stockings and a suspender belt. Agatha purchased these, along with a musquash coat, a wool dress, and a pleated skirt. Then she tried on the Georgette evening gown, the same model as the one in the window. The dress was apricot, and wonderfully suited Agatha's peach-white skin and auburn hair.

"You look beautiful, madam," said the manager. "I do agree," Evelyn Crawley said. She had admired the Georgette dress on display and had walked into the shop to have a look around. Her own cloth coat and felt hat were obviously inexpensive.

Agatha smiled at her. "Just the frock for Harrogate." Then she went back into the cubicle to change. "Don't let me monopolize the shop," Agatha called to Evelyn Crawley. "Am I keeping you waiting?"

"Not at all" came the answer. "My treatment isn't for some time. After that I've nothing to do till five, when a gentleman of sixty-three has asked me to tea. He thinks he can seduce me because I have the wrong sort of accent."

Agatha gave her jumper blouse a tug over her head and came out of the cubicle. "Good gracious, Miss Crawley, how awful."

Evelyn laughed. "Typical Harrogate, really. That's why I work in Bradford. I don't get so bad-tempered there. Nobody's posh." Evelyn picked up a slip that buttoned between the legs.

The manager said, "Those are Milanese Cami-Combs, madam."

"Well, they're certainly not Yorkshire."

Agatha giggled. The manager began to pack up the purchases.

Agatha turned to Evelyn Crawley. "May I ask you a favor? Could I possibly come with you to the baths? You know the form, and . . ."

"Of course." Evelyn smiled her dancing smile. "I'll introduce you to my therapist. She's the best and, as it's out of season, there'll be no problem fitting you in." Agatha felt grateful to the north-country girl. She thanked her warmly, then paid for her purchases in cash. The manager held up Agatha's muddied clothes, those in which she had arrived.

"Shall I wrap these with the rest?"

"No, thank you," Agatha said. "Throw them away."

Evelyn could not restrain an expression of surprise, although she was too polite to comment. Instead, she helped Agatha pick up her parcels and carry them out into the sun. Together they walked along the trim Edwardian Street, past the Palace Theatre, where a billboard advertised Gladys Cooper and Ivor Novello in *The Bohemian Girl*. Agatha stopped to read the small print. " 'British officers rescued by gypsies from Austrian soldiers,' " she recited. "Shall we go one night?"

"Oh, that would be nice," Evelyn Crawley said. She guessed that the invitation had required a certain courage on the part of her shy companion, who spoke very little on their way back to the hotel.

The parcels were left with the porter, and the two women set out for the Royal Baths, a formidable Victorian building some ten minutes' walk from the Hydro, the center of all spa operations. Because it was out of season, there were few guests, and horse-drawn carriages and bath chairs stood empty outside the building. Inside, elderly visitors and patients promenaded or sat at small tables in the vast entrance hall. Under the dome was an octagonal counter behind which a clerk took appointments, and, behind the clerk, blue mermaids cast in Royal Doulton china dove and soared. The dome of the huge entrance room was supported by Corinthian columns and the place was decorated with potted palms, fine-colored floor tiles, and the busts of local dignitaries.

Around the frieze, an inscription printed in huge letters read:

Ah what avail the largest gifts of heaven
When drooping Health and spirits go amiss,
How tasteless then whatever can be given,
Health is the vital principle of bliss and
Exercise of Health.

Agatha began immediately to reshape the verse in her head. "Scans poorly," she said aloud. She was a passionate amateur poet. As Mrs. Teresa Neele, her face carefully painted, she could be more adventurously herself than she had ever allowed before.

Evelyn Crawley stood next to Agatha and behind two frail and elderly people who took some considerable time booking their appointments.

"Are they here for the mud baths?" Agatha whispered.

"Yes. Several of the old things drown each year."

"Marinate in mud?"

"That's right. Poor old chucks."

The two elderly people wheeled themselves off and Evelyn and Agatha stepped forward to the desk. The clerk, a bloodless-looking man, recognized Evelyn.

"Yes, Miss Crawley?" He bared his teeth in a token smile. Then he looked down at his book. "Mrs. Braithwaite should be ready for you any minute now."

"I'd like this lady to take my appointment with her instead of me. Could you ask Mrs. Braithwaite to come to the desk?"

"Well, it's not customary to change appointments."

"Not customary, but not against the rules. Also, Mrs. Neele is in great pain. She'll book further appointments after she's had her consultation."

"Very good," said the clerk without enthusiasm.

"He doesn't really suit those mermaids, does he?" Agatha said as they walked away. They sat down to wait for the therapist.

"What else can you do, what other treatments are there?"

"Let me see." Evelyn thought. "Douches. Aeration baths. Scotch baths are fun. First you get boiled, then they shoot cold jets of water at you. Mrs. Braithwaite approves, but then she's a Scot. If you ask her about it, she'll smile and say, 'We pioneered it!' "

"She sounds rather a tartar."

"Not at all. She's very jolly. You'll like her, I'm sure of it."

"What else is there on the menu then?"

"The waters, of course. You're meant to drink gallons every day, different kinds of water for different complaints. Sulphur's most popular. It smells foul, tastes terrible. My mother used to call it 'frankly tonic.' You can imagine what she meant."

Agatha laughed. "Sort of purgatory."

"That's right. Then there are paraffin wax baths, which burn the skin, peat baths to suffocate you, and lots of electrical treatments, which Mrs. B. calls the 'nasties.' "

"What sort of thing?"

"The Galvanic bath, for example. That strengthens the muscles. The Bergonie chair. You can lose weight that way, too."

"You did say Harrogate wasn't a barrel of laughs, Miss Crawley."

"Quite true. You're a very inquiring sort of person."

"Oh, I don't think so."

"Yes, you are, and do call me Evelyn."

Agatha said, "I'm not very observant. I think it's because as a child I spent all my time daydreaming."

"Where did you live in South Africa?"

Agatha was momentarily at a loss for words. She looked across the vast room and then back to Evelyn. "Cape Town," she answered.

"You don't seem to have a South African accent."

"No, I was brought up in England. I do hope that therapist will agree to take me. I'm in agony."

Evelyn noticed that her friend obsessively stroked the gloves she had placed on the table. She was relieved when Mrs. Braithwaite arrived and she was able to introduce Mrs. Teresa Neele.

The therapist, who willingly agreed to substitute patients, was a staunch, middle-aged Scots lady and a devoted professional.

"Mrs. Neele has a very painful back," Evelyn explained.

"Well, we'll have to put that right."

"I think it's . . . spondylitis," Agatha said.

Mrs. Braithwaite was unimpressed. "Oh, yes, dear. A bad back."

"Will you be all right?" Evelyn asked. "Shall I wait for you?"

Agatha looked reassured.

"Tell you what," Evelyn said. "Meet me at

Betty's for lunch. It's second right around the corner."

"Yes, I will," Agatha said. "That would be lovely."

Mrs. Braithwaite led her patient along a low-ceilinged corridor into a complex of therapy rooms.

"We'll have a good look at that back, get you fit as a fiddle in no time."

They passed through a small room as bleak as a prison cell. In it was a bath stained brown and, attached to one wall, an elaborate system of coiled piping. The piping connected with a panel of clocks and dials.

"Now don't you worry about the nasties, Mrs. Neele. They're not as bad as they look."

"They look dreadful," Agatha said. She followed the therapist into another room, a room crowded with equipment and leather armchairs, a weighing machine, potted palms, and a desk behind which Mrs. Braithwaite sat to take notes.

Agatha's attention was fixed by a six-foot upright box with a seat inside and several dozen incandescent light bulbs.

"More nasties?" she asked.

"Reflector bulbs, my dear. Very therapeutic for arthritis. Now, some details, please. Apart from your back, any medical history I should know about?"

"No," Agatha answered.

Mrs. Braithwaite took her patient's pulse and blood pressure, handed her a white cotton gown, and told her to change in the adjacent room. When she had done so, Agatha was told to lie on the massage bed and lift each arm and leg in order that the therapist could determine which joints, muscles, and nerves were the cause of her problem.

"Head hanging over the end of the bed, Mrs. Neele. Good girl. Now stand up. Arms out to the side. Well done. Lift them slowly up above your head. That's right. A wee bit farther. Now turn the wrists around in circles. Does anything hurt?"

Agatha nodded. "In the small of my back it hurts."

"Touch your toes, Mrs. Neele." Agatha winced.

"Now sit here and hug the back of the chair. No, dear, back to front. Hold the back of the chair." Mrs. Braithwaite began to feel her way up her patient's spine. "Can't find anything wrong with your fifth lumbar. You're a tense person, Mrs. Neele. Muscles tied up in bunches. But I can't find anything seriously wrong. What you need is a nice Turkish bath and a good massage. Come along. Put on these slippers and follow me."

They went along a corridor, past patients in white gowns, and entered the Turkish baths, a vast partitioned area dominated by Moorish arches and colored tiles. At one end was a plunge pool in which several women were bathing. A therapist endeavored to hold up one geriatric who clearly could not swim and had begun to panic. At the other end was a heat room where women lay on slabs of marble to sweat.

"They look a bit like fish," Agatha said.

"Boiled fish, Mrs. Neele. Ten minutes of boiling for you."

After the heat treatment, Mrs. Braithwaite instructed her patient to shower and then began to massage her.

"My mother used to say, 'Jessica, my word, your hands are efficient. I don't know where you get the strength in your hands.' "

"Miss Crawley told me the Galvanic bath strengthens muscles," said Agatha. "Now that would help lose weight, too, wouldn't it?"

"Yes indeed. But you don't need that."

"I wouldn't have come to Harrogate if I hadn't wanted to take every advantage. When could I try the Galvanic bath?" The therapist was nonplused. "Well, normally, we give it to patients with serious muscular problems. It can be dangerous." She wiped off the excess oil from Agatha's back. "Now turn over, Mrs. Neele."

On her way to lunch, Agatha stopped at Smith's lending library and took out a subscription for one month. She selected two works of detective fiction, *The Phantom Train* and *The Double Thumb*. Then she went to meet her friend.

Evelyn watched Agatha devour a plate of small shrimps.

"You like shrimps and detective fiction," she said.

"I beg your pardon?"

"I'm trying to find out what you like." Evelyn paused. "I suppose that's impertinent. It's probably because I don't know anyone as . . . grand as you, who I can talk to."

"I'm awfully greedy about food, it's true."

"What else do you like?"

"Let me see. Expensive cars, pretty dresses, papier-mâché furniture. Dogs. I adore dogs. Lots of music. I like singing. Wanted to be an opera singer but I wouldn't have been good enough. What do you like, Evelyn?"

"I mostly *don't* like."

"What don't you like?"

"Chrysanthemums."

Agatha smiled. "What else?"

"The Prime Minister. He's always described as so wholesome. People say he smells of apples in the 'decadent atmosphere of postwar days.'"

"You're a modern girl."

"Oh, no. I don't like decadence much. All those girls in London with 'ravaged cigarettes.' I don't think they're probably very daring, though I haven't met any. How many of them would ride a camel?"

"Precisely!" Agatha said with feeling. And they both burst out laughing.

"Actually, I've ridden a camel and it was torture."

"I still envy you," Evelyn said.

"Then you should go to Egypt."

"I'll never be able to do that."

"Why ever not?"

"I'm a secretary, Teresa. It's not usual for a secretary to a Bradford mill manager to travel to Egypt."

Agatha was embarrassed. "How tactless of me," she said.

"Perhaps my tea date will buy me the ticket.

Trouble is, I've never had the nerve to take gifts from men."

"One couldn't possibly do that."

"Unless one was married. Then it's allowed," Evelyn said.

"Of course."

"No 'of course.' If I were married, I shouldn't wish to be kept."

"Oh, marriage isn't like that, Evelyn."

"For you, perhaps. You're special. Your husband must feel very fortunate."

Agatha's eyes filled with tears. "My husband's dead."

Evelyn stretched out her hand. "My dear, I'm so sorry."

"Do you mind if we go?"

They walked out of the restaurant, down to Crescent Gardens, and up the hill to their hotel, and although it was still early afternoon the sun was down and everything mushroom-dark.

Agatha said, "I'd like your help. I'm looking for my relatives. I've been considering placing an advertisement in the *Times* personal column. How about this: 'Will friends and relatives of Mrs. Teresa Neele, late of South Africa, please communicate.' Then a box number. Is that all I need to say?"

"I think that's fine, Teresa. But can't you contact your relatives more . . . directly?"

"You see, it's been so long since I was in England. Most of my family came from Rickmansworth, in Hertfordshire. They may well have moved."

"Yes, of course," Evelyn said reassuringly. She could make no sense of her friend's excessive agitation. Being a person of independent character, she could not imagine an indiscriminate need for relatives. She was fond of her family but thought them hopelessly servile. She rarely visited her parents, who had retired to the country. She found their demands on life too meager. Only her beloved grandmother, with whom she lived in Bradford, saw life with bright, critical, angry and imaginative eyes. It was her grandmother's example she wished to follow.

As the two women entered the hotel, two maids were busy putting up branches of pine and fir and holly.

"Do all the guests leave for Christmas?" Agatha asked.

"Most of them," Evelyn said, "except those that can't be carried out."

This remark did not cheer her friend, who seemed once more on the brink of tears. Evelyn took her arm. "You should post off your advertisement. Now it may take some time to make contact with your relatives. Perhaps you'd like to come and stay with us for Christmas. With my grandmother. She's not at all your world, Teresa. She has the broadest Yorkie accent you ever heard, but I think she'd make you laugh."

"That would be lovely," Agatha said. "If things aren't resolved."

As they crossed the lobby to the porter's desk, another guest, a rather gross man in his forties, lowered his newspaper and stared at Agatha with undisguised interest. Evelyn noticed the man, saw her friend react to this unnerving attention by lifting the collar of her coat as if she were a fugitive.

Chapter 5

Wally parked his car outside the Rickmansworth villa. On the gate of the semi-detached house in baroque lettering was painted "Rheola." He knocked at the front door. A middle-aged woman opened it.

"I'm looking for Mrs. Charles Neele."

"I'm Mrs. Neele," the woman replied. "What can I do for you?"

"I'm from the *Globe-Enquirer*, Wally Stanton."

The woman nervously asked him to come in.

"Awfully sorry to trouble you, Mrs. Neele, but I'm investigating the disappearance of Mrs. Christie. I thought perhaps your daughter might be able to help. She is Colonel Christie's secretary?"

"Yes. But my daughter's on holiday at the moment."

"Can you tell me where she is?"

"No, Mr. Stanton. I'm sure you'll understand. But with all this . . . this . . ."

"Embarrassment?"

"Yes, that's right. Nancy wishes to keep her whereabouts secret."

"Do you have any theories about Mrs. Christie's disappearance?"

"Well, my husband and I feel she must have lost her memory. You know, she wasn't well."

"And you don't think the cause of her disappearance had anything to do with . . . ? We've received rumors that the Colonel and your daughter were on very familiar terms."

"Nothing could be further from the truth. The fact is that both I and my husband know Colonel Christie and his wife. Nancy is a friend of both Colonel and Mrs. Christie. Some months ago, she stayed with the Christies for the weekend, so you see your rumors are quite without foundation."

Mrs. Neele completed her ingenuous explanation with a smile. Wally had the strongest feeling she had rehearsed it carefully, no doubt after consultation with the Colonel.

He thanked the woman and turned to leave.

An hour later, Wally drove up to Mrs. Helmsley's house in Dorking. He was told by a servant that the Colonel's mother was not at home. However, when he telephoned the house from a nearby public booth, Mrs. Helmsley answered and agreed to speak to him. When asked about her daughter-in-law's disappearance, she said it could well be explained by a loss of memory "because of emotional stress and depression. Indeed, last Friday afternoon Mrs. Christie visited me and told me of a temporary loss of memory she'd suffered while driving."

Wally thanked her for her help.

Nancy Neele had been waiting at the entrance to King's Cross Station for some time before Archie Christie drew up in a cab. As he got out and paid his fare, another taxi drew up and deposited John Foster on the pavement. In the service of Wally Stanton, John had not let the Colonel out of his sight. He hastily paid off his cabbie and followed Nancy and Archie. Preceded by a porter carrying Nancy's two suitcases, they made their way into the station to the first-class-ticket booth.

"One return to Harrogate, please," Archie said. He paid for the ticket and then the little group, led by the porter and tagged by John, continued toward the platform. John heard Nancy say, "I wish I weren't going," and the Colonel reply, "It's for the best. Your aunt will look after you. If the press find out you've canceled a holiday, anything out of the ordinary . . . Heaven knows, they may have tailed me here."

At that moment Nancy and Archie went past the ticket barrier and John, who had not had time to purchase a platform ticket, lost them.

Archie continued. "Do you understand, Nancy? If they print anything about you and me . . . it would be disastrous." He pulled forward his hat as if to avoid recognition. "I'd have to leave the firm." They followed the porter along the platform. "I shan't be able to come up, y'know."

Tears filled Nancy's eyes. "You said you were going to leave her."

"I am," he said. "That is, I want to marry you but . . ." Archie dropped his voice as the porter approached for a tip. "Decently," he added for Nancy's benefit.

Nancy climbed onto the train and Archie followed her into the empty carriage where the porter had deposited her luggage.

"I don't think you'll ever leave Agatha," Nancy said.

"Of course I will," Archie said. "I love you." But he did not reassure his girl. She was not a complicated sort of person, nor was she stupid. She recognized in Archie a great fear of public disapproval and knew it to be the major threat to her happiness.

"Has Agatha killed herself?"

"Of course not," he said. "I think she's up to something. Whatever it is, it's to wound me." He sat down, head bent in misery.

"Perhaps she loves you," Nancy said.

"Loves me! She wants my blood."

"Or wants you back," Nancy said gently. She sat down beside him, put her hand in his.

"You'd better go," she told him.

Wally Stanton sat drinking in a Fleet Street pub which, because of its drabness, drew none of the journalists and lawyers to whom that part of London belonged. It was a private, cosy sort of place where threadbare men and even some women came when they could afford the comfort of a drink. The walls were the color of brown ale, and a coal fire was always kept burning.

It was midday on Tuesday, December seventh, and Wally had become preoccupied with the disappearance of Agatha Christie. He was not alone; the story had now reached the front pages of the national newspapers. But Wally had done his sleuthing a little more thoroughly than his colleagues.

He took out his notebook and headed a clean page:

(1) Family Point of View: Colonel Christie.

Underneath he transcribed a quotation from the previous page: "My wife discussed some time ago the possibility of engineering her disappearance and said she could disappear at will if she liked. That shows that the possibility of engineering her disappearance, possibly in connection with her work, was running through her mind." He added a further statement of Archie's from another newspaper: "The only explanation I can offer for her disappearance is that she had a nervous breakdown and is suffering from loss of memory."

Then he wrote:

Mrs. Helmsley and Mrs. Neele: loss of memory.

Wally sipped his whiskey and water and wrote:

(2) Fiction: Family—sincerely or not—offers two explanations for novelist's disappearance. Both happen to have been skillfully employed by Mrs. Christie in her fiction.

Wally had come to this conclusion by diligent effort. He had discovered a novel of Mrs. Christie's, *The Secret Adversary*, in which the heroine, Jane Finn, successfully feigns complete loss of memory for a considerable period as a means of getting out of a dangerous situation. In a collection of short stories he had found *The Disappearance of Mr. Davenheim,* in which Poirot explains to his Watson-type friend that there are three types of disappearance: the voluntary type, the real loss-of-memory case, and, last, murder. Had the ingenious lady, Wally wondered, planted clues to all three possibilities?

Or perhaps the family simply felt loss of memory to be the least embarrassing explanation for the disappearance of their wayward relative. There remained, of course, Kenward's dogged loyalty to the idea of foul play.

Wally wrote down:

(3) Mistress.

He ordered another drink.

The publican brought over Wally's whiskey.

"Looking a bit under the weather, Mr. Stanton," he said.

"I'm looking for a lady, Reg."

"Thought you was good at that kind of thing, sir."

"A lady detective writer, Reg. Called Christie."

"Oh 'er. If you believe what you read in the papers, there are dozens of Agatha Christies skulking around the country. Tell you one thing. They wouldn't be running after my missus if she disappeared." He gave his ear a good scratch. "Nor would I, for that matter. Now what can I offer you, a nice steak and kidney pudding?"

At that moment John Foster came charging into the pub, hair on end, eyes wild, bumping through the crowd and roaring in his excitement. "Ho, ho! Have I got a story!"

The events at King's Cross were described for Wally's benefit.

"You're the tops, John," said Wally solemnly. "Got your hooks into this story. Of course, it might have been wise to follow the mistress."

John looked crestfallen. "But you told me to stick with the Colonel."

"Quite true, I did. Now don't print a word of it till we know more."

"Not on your life!" John said.

Wally broke into his steak and kidney pudding. "I'm trying to make sense of it, John, and I can't. Family says she's lost her memory and wandered off. Your Kenward believes she's dead. Is he a fool?"

"Old Bill's not a fool," John said.

"Well, my dear Watson, you get the hell down there and try and find out what he knows that we don't."

As the two men got up to leave, a shabby, toothless spinster greeted Wally.

"Hello, Violet," he said.

"Afternoon, Wally. How about a beer?"

He bought the old woman a drink. "Got to go now."

She continued to hold him by the sleeve. "I've got a story for you, Wally. You know how when I go to sleep my other self doesn't half carry on?"

Wally nodded patiently.

"Remember when she saw this huge fire? And the time she saw a lady lift up a huge chopper and plunge it into somebody's back?"

"Yes, Violet."

"Have to be in the right frame of mind," she went on, "healthy and that, or it don't happen. Last night my other self was dancing with this fellow with spectacles. When we began to talk, his spectacles broke, and . . ." She looked up at Wally, suddenly baffled and unhappy. "And I couldn't see him."

Wally gently removed her hand. "See you tomorrow," he said, and walked out into the street with John.

"Watson?"

"Yes?"

"I've a clue, real humdinger sort of a clue," Wally said. "It just came to me."

Lord Dintworth, proprietor of the *Globe-Enquirer*, strode across the newsroom to his editor's office. Henry Dintworth was a sixty-year-old man with a patrician face and the habit of power.

He nodded to Briggs, the newspaper's editor, and examined a desk covered with photographs of Agatha Christie—Agatha at her desk, in her drawing room, and on the golf course.

"Taken three years ago," Briggs explained. He pointed out some others. "These are recent, a literary luncheon last week."

Dintworth glanced at a few newspaper reports and checked the mock-up of the *Globe-Enquirer*'s headline for the following morning—FAMOUS AUTHORESS: NATIONWIDE SEARCH. Underneath was a photograph of the Silent Pool and, in the foreground, Kenward surrounded by reporters. The proprietor examined the picture closely, then turned on his editor. "For God's sake, who sent Wally down there?"

"Wally sent himself. It's more than a news story, don't you think?"

Dintworth picked up the photographs of Archie Christie and threw them into the wastebasket.

"No pictures of the Colonel."

Briggs looked surprised. "I think Wally could make something of this disappearance, or whatever it is," he said. "He's read her books, he's got some inside stuff from the local Sunningdale reporter. He's got to the family."

"I didn't bring Wally over here at huge personal expense for this! Out of the question."

"He can make this kind of story sell like hot cakes."

Briggs's plea was interrupted by the sound of static over the office intercom, followed by the voice of a newscaster: " 'The fact that the trade unions have become the tool of the Socialist party,' said Winston Churchill, 'has brought politics into industry in a manner hitherto unknown in any country.' "

The newscaster's voice continued, but slowed, as if from a wound-down gramophone. " '. . . although the majority of trade unionists wish to be good citizens of the country and Empire . . .' "

There followed the sound of a loud raspberry. Lord Dintworth turned angrily and crossed the newsroom in the direction of his office. Over the intercom came the sound of a tinny horn playing "Land of Hope and Glory." Baffled reporters looked up from their desks and smiled.

Lord Dintworth's office was conservative and luxurious. Wally Stanton sat at the huge desk. In front of him was a banner headline that read CHURCHILL SPEAKS OUT. As his editor walked in, Wally cupped his hands once more over his mouth and blew into the intercom a simulated horn solo of "I'm Just Wild About Harry."

Dintworth got his anger under control and crossed his office. Immediately Wally jumped up and bowed elaborately.

"The entertainment! From across the seas."

The proprietor sat down in his own chair. "I want you to interview Henry Ford. He's just arrived and we can get an exclusive. Lead story for the column, yes?"

Wally smiled. "I've done him, years ago. I squeezed no juice out of that lemon."

"Listen, Wally. Ford's a friend, and he's been praising British workmen."

"Nice of him, but I have a story, Harry, and you'll like it."

"You can't do it. Why the devil did you go down to that Silent Pool or whatever it's called?"

Wally paused. "Did you know Christie has a mistress? Local reporter on the *Echo* found out she's gone to Harrogate."

"I want no mention of the mistress."

Wally went on patiently. "Christie has a mother who says our novelist has lost her memory. And Agatha Christie recently wrote a story about a faked amnesia. That was a good story and so is this."

Dintworth opened his desk diary. He said

calmly, "Home Office rang. Very high up in the Government. Knows the Christies. Asked me not to mention the mistress."

Wally smiled as he always did to cover feelings of anger and distaste. He imitated the proprietor's voice: "Government says war has been declared but we'd rather you didn't . . ."

"Story's not worth the trouble, dear boy. Leave it to the news boys."

Wally pulled out his notebook. He read aloud: " 'A voluntary disappearance . . . may be so cleverly staged as to be exceedingly puzzling—especially if, as here, we are concerned with a very skillful writer of detective stories whose mind has been trained in the study of ways and means to perplex.' Now that's Dorothy L. Sayers."

"Who?"

"Sayers. She's a famous writer. Detective fiction, same kind of stuff as Mrs. Christie."

Dintworth took up his fountain pen and began to sign letters. "Write about whatever else you want but not this."

"You sent me to that lunch," said Wally. "I saw Mrs. Christie. Heard some private stuff. She's in trouble. And the family's covering up!"

"I won't print it."

Wally lost his temper. "It can now be revealed that King George's favorite dish is rice pudding. Though Lord Dintworth is excited, the public is remaining calm."

"I find that rather offensive, Wally Odd, really, because I've always found you quite well-mannered." He looked up. "For an American."

Wally smiled. "Very odd. But quite good for circulation."

△

It was quite early in the morning and Agatha had taken breakfast in bed. She was surrounded by newspapers. One of them carried an interview with Archie which quoted him as saying "I'm very worried, very harassed." Another had a banner headline: MISSING NOVELIST—WIDESPREAD SEARCH FOR MRS. CHRISTIE. Underneath the headline three identical photographs of her face had been given three different hair styles. A smaller caption read: "Possible Disguises Adopted by the Author."

Agatha got out of bed and held up the newspaper to the looking glass so she could compare the photographs with her own appearance. She was reassured to see that there was only the slightest resemblance. Her eye slipped down the page to an advertisement that read: "A rose petal complexion. How to keep it." She read the details carefully; then she started to make up her face, to apply creamy rouge and pale powder. She put on a dressing gown and sat down at the writing table.

Out of her hand valise, Agatha took some strips of paper held together by elastic. On the top of one she wrote in capital letters: LOSS OF MEMORY: ARCHIE. On the second: FOUL PLAY: POLICE VIEW. On the third she wrote: VICTIM.

She held the third strip for a moment, then put it with the others. On a clean piece of paper she wrote, "The woman began to choke on the piece of meat. Her eyes bulged and her face went blue.

Her body heaved and her throat rasped in great
rhythmic cataclysmic shrugs."

She reread this, then scrunched it up and threw
it into the basket.

On a fresh sheet she wrote:

1. Isolated place
2. Bizarre death
3. Accomplice (s)
4. Red herrings
5. Winner/loser

Her concentration was broken by a knock on
the bedroom door. She called "Come in" while
putting the strips and sheets of paper into her
case.

Flora, the chambermaid, came in bearing some
fresh laundry. She glanced around the room,
hugely curious, at the hat boxes and the books,
the bowl of apples, the expensive dress lying over
an armchair.

"Looks like you'll be staying some time, Mrs.
Neele."

"Oh, I hope so, Flora."

"Have they found your luggage?"

"No, not yet, I'm afraid."

"The chef's got a brother in South Africa."

"Oh, really. Now, could you get me a copy of
today's *Times*?"

"Yes, ma'am, of course."

"Thank you, Flora."

Agatha turned her back to dismiss the maid and
opened her library copy of *Hydrotherapy in Britain*. She began to make notes in a new exercise
book. She wrote:

1. Mineral waters—pure chalybeates, and alkaline sulphur.

She read on, then added:

Would strong taste disguise the addition of a drug?
2. Bathing: 34 seconds complete emersion.

She copied out the following from the book:

3. "Galvanic current as used in bath and Schnee chair. Current intensity is slowly increased by moving up the handle on the shunt rheostat. Current flows from a terminal through the electrodes hanging in the water of the baths, through the patient and back to terminal b below handle of rheostat, and re-enters mains through terminal c."

Agatha closed the exercise book and dropped it into her small case. She locked the case and put the key in her handbag.

She selected an apple from the fruit bowl on the table and began to munch it. She munched apples as other writers smoked cigarettes or stroked a cat or fingered beads.

Two hours later Agatha kept her second appointment with Mrs. Braithwaite in Therapy Room 4 of the Royal baths. In one corner was a bath connected to a central instrument panel. This panel was also wired to a curious-looking chair, half hidden by a screen.

As in the consulting room, the carpets and potted palms provided reassuring contrast to the fearful-looking equipment. Mrs. Braithwaite, starched and comforting, told Agatha to undress and put on a gown in the changing room next door. She ran warm water into the bath and, when her patient returned, told her to get in.

"You really don't need the Galvanic, my dear. But, since you insisted . . . Now lie back against the wooden frame and keep your arms in the water. Ready?"

"Yes, ready."

The therapist set the rheostat and flipped the switch. Agatha felt a mild tingling sensation caused by a series of tiny spasms set off at regular intervals and increasing in intensity.

"How strong can it be?" she asked.

"You don't want it too strong. The current activates the muscles. Overdo it, and you'd cause muscular cramp."

"Muscular cramp's not serious, is it?"

"It can be, my dear," said Mrs. Braithwaite. "The heart can be damaged. We have to be very careful with electricity, especially through water." She examined the clock on the wall. "Now that's enough for today."

After she was dressed, Agatha made her way to the octagonal desk in the great entrance hall of the building to book further treatments. The clerk asked for her name.

"Mrs. Neele. Miss Crawley introduced us, and I'd like to make my appointments." She handed the man Mrs. Braithwaite's note. He thumbed through his book.

"Mrs. Teresa Neele," Agatha repeated. "N, double e, l, e. It's an unusual name. You won't have any others."

The clerk glanced down at his list. "We have a

Miss Nancy Neele booked. Spelt the same way, as
a matter of fact." The man produced the information smugly.

"When is Miss Neele booked in?" Agatha asked.

"Thursday morning, midday," he replied.

"I shall have to get in touch with her; we may
be related."

But the clerk was no longer interested and
turned his attention to the next patient.

Agatha had promised the afternoon to her new
friend. When they met, Evelyn gave her a prettily
wrapped box.

"Farrah's Original," she said.

"Original what?"

"Toffee. Shop's been selling it for donkey's
years."

"Thank you," Agatha said. "I'm very grateful."

"Now it's Pierrots. But we have to walk."

Agatha laughed. "I'm in your charge."

"There's nothing in this town worth a penny
damn except for toffee and Pierrots," Evelyn said
with her usual conviction.

"You do know your mind, Evelyn."

"You mean I'm opinionated. Everybody says
that. When I was fourteen, my mum decided to
have me prepared for confirmation. She was a
right snob and thought the Church of England a
cut above us Methodists. She sent me along to an
irritable old clergyman. I kept on asking 'But
why?' about everything till the minister lost his
temper and said I'd have to wait another year, that
God would come to me in His own fashion, which
He didn't."

"Didn't you try the next year?"

"No. That year my mother found another way of improving my position in the world. She sent me to secretarial college. It was a much better idea—cost her a penny, but I suppose it was worth it." Evelyn looked at Agatha's lapel, then looked again. "Have you had an unhappy love affair?"

Agatha looked startled.

"You always wear that brooch. Yellow tulip. It means hopeless love."

Agatha squinted down at her lapel. "That's ridiculous, Evelyn. My mother gave it to me. It was a present to her from my father, and *their* marriage was perfect."

"That's nice," Evelyn said. "Anyway, I suppose it's foolish to believe in that kind of symbol."

The two women crossed Valley Gardens till they reached the Magnesia Well, a pretty Victorian rotunda. A group of people, among them several courting couples, some children, a number of old people warmly wrapped for the weather, had made a circle around the Harrogate Pierrots. The four aged performers wore shabby Harlequin suits with ruffled collars. They had painted lips, blackened arched eyebrows, and white make-up that had settled into the creases of their faces, lined by the long effort to please.

"Ooh! Talk about sailors and ships! Oh, what an experience!" said one of the men. And the routine went like this:

"What?"

"I've just come off the ship, never been so embarrassed in me life."

"Why were you embarrassed?"

"There I was, coming through the Customs, both arms around my case, and do you know what?"

"No, what?"

"I felt my trousers dropping down."

"And what did you do?"

"Ooh, I didn't know what to do. I didn't know whether to drop the case or drop me trousers."

"And what did you do?"

"I dropped me trousers!"

"And what about the case?"

"It's coming up next Thursday!"

The audience laughed, and Evelyn and Agatha clapped enthusiastically.

The four Pierrots touched their knees and squeaked, "Ooooh!"

"They're *wonderful*," Agatha said. "Reminds me of Pierrots on the pier."

"In South Africa?"

"Yes," she answered vaguely.

The four performers struck up "All the Nice Girls Love a Sailor," and the audience joined in.

Across the circle Agatha caught sight of Nancy Neele, who was holding the arm of an elderly woman. She noticed how young Nancy looked, and thought her coat was expensive.

Evelyn said, "What ever's the matter? You're as white as a sheet." She looked across the circle to where Agatha's attention seemed to be fixed. "Is that girl someone you know?"

Agatha turned and walked quickly away. Her friend ran after her.

"I think she might be a relative, Evelyn. Looks just like one of my cousins."

"Well, would you like to . . . uh . . . speak to her?"

"No, I couldn't possibly do that. I might be wrong."

Evelyn was baffled by this eccentric reaction, by the strange change of mood. They walked away in silence.

"I'm so sorry," Agatha apologized. "I had a *lovely* time. Haven't had such a nice time for . . ."

"Donkey's years," Evelyn said in a disparaging way, as if to cover for the inadequacy of her offering.

"Yes, for ages," Agatha said.

When they reached their hotel, they parted company. Agatha went to the telephone booth in the lobby. She asked the operator to put her through to the Valencia Hotel. She asked the receptionist there how long Nancy Neele had been in Harrogate. Then she hung up without leaving a message.

Later that evening, Agatha joined Evelyn Crawley in the Hydro Winter Garden, a glass-ceilinged conservatory supported by elegant iron columns. In the center was a fountain and around the room were many small tables and wicker chairs and palm trees and statues of buxom ladies holding up lamps. Dividing the Winter Garden from the ballroom was a podium on which the Hydro Band performed. It consisted of piano, violin, banjo, and sax. A mere half-dozen guests occupied the ballroom. One couple had taken the floor: an elderly lady was having an uncomfortable time with an un-co-ordinated enthusiast of around twenty.

Agatha and Evelyn watched the couple with

some glee from a table on the Winter Garden side of the podium, just below the orchestra.

"What a curious-looking boy. Wonder why he's here."

"That's Oscar Jones," Evelyn said. "He looks after his uncle." She pointed. "That old geezer in the wheelchair. Owns a ball-bearing factory in Manchester. No family except his nephew. Oscar hopes Uncle Jones will die soon so he can take off to London with his inheritance. He wants to join the chorus of the D'Oyly Carte opera company. Talks only of Gilbert and Sullivan."

"Doesn't sound like a very expensive ambition. Does he have to wait?"

"I think he thinks you have to buy your way into the company," Evelyn said. "He's very eccentric."

She poured some brandy into her coffee cup from a flask that she kept in her handbag. She offered some to Agatha, who refused. "I don't like the taste. Rather like you not caring for chrysanthemums." She opened a newspaper and folded it to turn up the crossword puzzle.

"What *do* you like, Evelyn, apart from Pierrots and your grandmother?"

"I don't like my gran when she says 'You have a good pair of eyes.' Rather as if I were lucky not to have three. That's her way of saying 'Why don't you have a young man?'"

"Well, isn't she right?"

"No, she's not. I do. But I can't marry him and I don't think I really want to." Evelyn poured some more brandy into her cup. "He's already married, though I don't think that's the point. I don't think I'd like the . . . encroachment, if you know what I mean, if I were married. I wouldn't want to be pinned down."

Agatha leaned forward. "But that's what's so nice about marriage, the companionship and the fun. That is, if you love with a whole heart."

"You're a woman of means," Evelyn said, "aren't you? You could *afford* to love with a whole heart."

Agatha half listened, half turned into herself. She said in a harsh voice, "You must do what you can, not what you can't. Unless, of course, you have a terrific will."

Evelyn emptied some more from her flask into her cup. Her friend was disturbing. "You have *very* angry hair," she blurted out, and was immediately embarrassed by her candor. "I think I've had too much brandy," she added.

Agatha looked down at her crossword puzzle to block out the remark.

"All right. What's a slave to a stockbroker?"

"A bondman," said Evelyn promptly.

Agatha smiled. "Have some more brandy."

She looked up at the musicians as they began to play Saint-Saëns's "Softly Awakes My Heart."

"That's the first proper sing I learned at the conservatory."

"Sing it, Teresa."

"I don't think they'd"—Agatha looked around the room at the staid geriatrics—"approve."

"Go on. I dare you," said her friend.

Agatha walked up to the pianist.

"Do you think I might sing this with you?" The pianist had not had such a request for a decade, and he looked to his leader for confirmation.

"We'd be delighted," he said.

Standing just below the dais, Agatha sang in a small, sweet, soprano voice:

> "Softly awakes my heart
> As the flowers awaken
> To Aurora's tender Zephyr.
> But say, O well-be-lov'd, no more
> I'll be for-sak-en . . ."

Chapter 6

The winter field near Newlands Corner was so frozen that the earth clods were as hard as paving stones and tripped up many a luckless reporter and policeman and voluntary helper who had come out in search of the missing novelist. It was the sixth day of the Christie disappearance, and Superintendent Kenward had called in the help of the Guildford and Shere Beagles. He himself found it difficult to keep pace with the pink-coated masters of the hunt as they sprinted after the beagle hounds. The dogs had been provided with a shoe and some clothing of Mrs. Christie's to put them on the scent.

Wally Stanton stood watching Kenward's sporting maneuver with growing irritation. He had come to meet John Foster, and Foster had not yet shown up. Wally was not going to go along with his employer's refusal to allow him to cover the story. He would sell it elsewhere, he'd sell it back home. The problem was that he wasn't getting anywhere. Part of his determination to keep going was inspired by John Foster's being sacked from the *Sunningdale Echo*. Foster had been told by his editor that he had got to go, that people in high places had complained he had made "unwarrantable intrusions" into the Christie affair. The editor, a timorous man, allowed no argument.

So Wally took the baffled and humiliated young man under his wing, promised him a stipend, told him that somehow or other they would get the story and sell it. The idea of joining forces with so eminent a journalist as Wally Stanton spurred John to intensive efforts.

Superintendent Kenward had informed the press that of all the bizarre cases with which he had been associated, the Christie one was the most baffling. The baffling part to the constabularies of the other three counties involved in the search was Kenward's conviction that Mrs. Christie's body would be found in the vicinity of Newlands Corner.

The word went around that old Bill was carrying stubbornness to the point of lunacy. Kenward told the reporters Mrs. Christie had driven into London from Sunningdale at about three o'clock on Saturday morning, and then motored back. "I have reason to believe that she passed through Shere at four A.M." He refused to divulge any more information.

Meanwhile, respected members of the press corps had followed up other leads. Wally questioned his colleagues.

"Some fellow found a powder puff, thought it

belonged to Mrs. Christie. So he gave it to a clairvoyant and she said the body would be found in a log cabin."

"And was it?" Wally asked.

"Young fellow from the *Westminster Gazette* found a log cabin near here. East Clandon. Broke in. Guess what he found?"

"Beyond my scope," said Wally.

"Well, he found a bottle of opium and a postcard. Only one word could be deciphered and that was 'dale.' "

"Gosh," said Wally.

"They laid down a layer of powder and this morning there were footsteps imprinted."

"Footsteps belonged to a lady painter," Wally said, "and it wasn't opium. It was for diarrhea."

He moved forward with the little band of reporters toward Kenward, who was returning with his men across the frozen field.

"Dogs found the body?" asked a disgruntled old crime reporter.

"What we want to know about is Captain Campbell Christie's letter from Mrs. Christie."

Wally moved closer. "What letter?" he asked.

"Missed a trick, Mr. Stanton? She told her brother-in-law she was going to a Yorkshire spa."

"When was it posted?"

"From London," Kenward answered. "The morning after she disappeared."

The old reporter grinned. "And the police go beagling in Surrey."

Kenward said patiently, "I think Mrs. Christie posted her letter, then drove back to Sunningdale.

She'd already told her secretary to cancel her trip to Beverley, in Yorkshire."

"What if she changed her mind?" Wally asked.

"Police have followed up all the leads in the north," Kenward said. "Checked the hotels at all the major spas. She isn't registered."

"Perhaps she used another name?" somebody suggested.

Kenward suddenly shouted, "Mrs. Christie isn't there! She's here."

Wally asked, "So you think Campbell Christie gave out details to put you off the scent?"

"There were other letters," said the police officer and turned his back.

The group of frozen and dissatisfied sleuths began to move off. "Most talked-about woman in the country," one of them said. "Probably disappeared as a publicity stunt."

"Not that lady," Wally said, with more conviction than he had any reasonable right to feel.

"How the hell would you know?" the reporter replied. "Bloody Yank!"

Wally lifted his hat in mock civility and made for the road.

From the top of the hill came John Foster, running and stumbling over the earth, panting up to Wally, unable to get the words out, his arms going up and down like distress signals.

"I've cracked . . . Ke-Kenward!" He paused to get his breath.

"Okay, take it easy."

"A letter . . ."

"I know about the letter, John."

"The one to Kenward?"

"Take your time."

"Grummit—works for the Superintendent—spilled the beans. It took cunning, Wally. Took skill. Had to go to town on that old snob."

"Don't doubt that, John."

"Told her you wanted to meet her."

"Jesus, John. So what did she spill?"

"There was another letter. Addressed to Kenward, posted Friday night and he got it on Saturday at the station. Know who signed it? Mrs. bloody Christie! Grummit thinks Mrs. Christie felt threatened."

Wally patted John on the shoulder. "Well done, old chap. Well done." He sounded more enthusiastic than he felt. "And that explains Kenward's view."

"That she's dead?"

"No, that she's alive, if it's genuine."

John blinked. Wally smiled at him. "Going to have to double your fee, John. Well done."

At about eleven o'clock that evening, Wally arrived at the 53 Club with his secretary, Polly, on his arm. He was immediately greeted by the manager.

"Good evening, Mr. Stanton."

"Lord Dintworth in?" Wally asked, taking off his hat and scarf.

"Yes, he is. Usual table."

The art deco room they entered was the most popular London nightclub of that month. The orange and jade-green room was uncomfortably crowded. Wally propelled his partner along a balcony and down across the dance floor to the other side of the room. Girls with bobbed and shingled hair, faces white, lips scarlet, figures thin as fronds, danced with dapper men in the latest-model dinner jacket. One girl, wearing a long rope of pearls and an armload of diamond bracelets, gave Wally an ecstatic unfocused smile. He steered Polly past her. "Cocaine—or does she think I'm pretty?"

"She thinks you're pretty."

They climbed the three steps to Lord Dintworth's large balcony table. "Want to join us?" he called out.

Wally found a couple of chairs and squeezed them in between Dintworth and a hard-faced woman in her fifties. He looked around the table. "The service is terrible, the food's inedible, but thank God it's expensive." There was polite laughter.

Dintworth indicated the hard-faced woman sitting to Wally's left. "Wally Stanton. The Duchess of Stoke, Lord Cublington." He enunciated the names of the other two guests at the table less clearly, as if they did not deserve the attention accorded to the titled.

The newspaper proprietor signaled to a waiter to bring drinks and turned to Lord Cublington. "Go on with the story." He leaned over to Polly. "Georgie's suffering from parental rebuke."

Cublington, a hugely fat young man, continued his story. "Knew there was going to be trouble when I got to his club. Glared at me through the soup and the pheasant. Then the old boy said, 'Laziness is the real enemy. From now on, make sure your feet touch the ground before your valet draws the curtains in the morning!' Then he bellowed, 'Now shut up and get on with your claret!' "

Cublington shook like a jelly and everybody else laughed.

Wally filled his own and Polly's glass from the bottle of whiskey on the table. The Duchess of Stoke turned to speak to him. "I do love your column. It's frightfully amusing."

Wally thanked her.

Dintworth interrupted. "How's Henry Ford?"

"He's fallen for Nancy Neele."

"Really," said the Duchess, who had never heard of Nancy Neele.

"Yep," Wally continued. "Hump-nutty about her."

Dintworth turned an angry smile on Polly. "Come here often?" he asked.

The girl had been watching the dance floor. "Pardon? Oh, no, it's the first time. It's ever so nice."

Her accent confirmed what the other people at the table had suspected from her dress: Polly wasn't one of them. She was thereafter ignored.

The Duchess pursued Wally. "You must find us rather quiet after America."

Wally adopted his earnest look. "No, I find England just as noisy. It's just a different kind of sound."

"I'm told all the gels in New York are buying up nigger maids to teach them how to Charleston."

"That's right," Wally said. "And all the fellas are up flagpoles. They just sit up there and don't come down."

"Rather clever of them!" roared Cublington across the table.

The young couple got up to dance, and George Cublington followed them with the Duchess on his arm.

Wally turned to Dintworth. "Listen, Harry. Did you have John Foster fired?"

Dintworth answered mildly. "I told you to leave it to the newsroom."

"I'll sell it elsewhere."

"No paper will mention the mistress."

"Unless the story's very good. If you want a highly paid whore, why won't you let me deliver?"

"Be reasonable, dear boy. It won't help you, this Christie story. I promise. You simply don't know how things work here."

"It'll sell your newspaper. There's a cover-up."

Dintworth shook his head. "Wouldn't do. Anyway, the Christie woman's a bloody nuisance, I'm told." He turned to Polly as if the conversation were at an end. Wally smiled. Very gently he removed the carnation from his own buttonhole, leaned forward, and stuck it behind Dintworth's ear. The press lord made a gesture as if to hit Wally, who stood up slowly, took Polly's hand, and walked toward the exit.

The two of them stood outside the club, and Polly hummed the tune that they could hear coming faintly from inside. "It's such a sad song," she said, ignoring the upset with their employer.

"But such a happy life," he answered. "If I could get it up."

The doorman came running back along the street. "Your car, sir?"

"Yes, and a cab."

Wally turned to the girl. "Polly, I'm going to send you home on your own. I've had too much to drink and I'm not fit for anyone tonight." When the cab drew up the girl got in. She smiled understandingly and was driven off. Wally knew he had hurt her. He felt bad about the girl, and about most of the rest of his life.

The doorman drove up in Wally's battered Morris. He held the door open for its owner while regarding the vehicle with some dismay. "These are hard times, sir." Wally began to laugh. He went on laughing while he tipped the doorman. Then he drove off at speed.

An hour later he lurched into the drive of Styles, got out of his car, and rang the doorbell. When there was no reply, he put his finger on the bell and kept it there. Several minutes later, lights went on inside the house.

Jane gingerly half opened the door. She recognized Wally and opened the door farther. Behind her, also wearing a dressing gown, was Charlotte Fisher.

"Who are you?" she demanded in a bold voice. The man in the dinner jacket weaved into the hall.

"I'm God," said Wally, "and I'm moving in a mysterious way. I want to see Colonel Christie."

Miss Fisher felt somewhat reassured. The man was drunk and therefore probably safe. "Colonel Christie isn't back yet," she said firmly. "Shall I wake the butler, or can I help?"

Wally looked at a loss. "Why do Englishmen always want to hit other Englishmen?"

Fisher said, in her most sensible voice, "Is that what they want to do?"

"Or their wives."

"Go to bed, Jane," she said, holding the front door open. "I think it's time you went, sir."

"May I ask who you are?"

"I'm Mrs. Christie's secretary. Now please go."

Wally looked her in the eye as steadily as he could manage. "Mrs. Christie's in trouble and her family's covering up."

The secretary turned hostile. "Who are you?"

"Wally Stanton." He enunciated very carefully. "I'm a newspaper columnist."

"Well, we don't want the press around here. You've caused enough pain as it is. Now please go."

Wally shook his head. Miss Fisher tried another tack. "Mrs. Christie's not been well," she explained in a kindly sort of way, as if to a child. "Her mother died recently. That's all there is to it."

"I want to know your name," he said.

"Charlotte Fisher. And if you don't go now, I'll call for help."

"Miss Fisher," he said in a defenseless way, "I badly need a cup of coffee."

"I'm sorry but—"

"I'm sorry, too, and I'm not going to hurt you. You'd fell me with one blow. But I'm not going to be able to get back to London in this condition without a cup of coffee."

He looked at her winningly. Charlotte Fisher gave in. "I'll make you some coffee if you promise to drink it quickly and go. Now follow me—and don't make a noise."

Wally sat at the scrubbed kitchen table in the white-tiled room while Miss Fisher warmed up the coffee. "Would you mind if I took my coat off, or would that make you angry again?"

She pursed her lips in a resigned sort of way and handed him the hot drink.

"A slug of milk would help," he said with a grin. She fetched some milk and stood over him while he sipped it. He was a lot more sober than he made out. "I get the feeling your lady's been blackballed, Miss Fisher. Kicked out of some nameless club. Are you part of that club?"

He could see he'd made a small incision in the secretary's armor.

"There is no club. We all want her back. Desperately."

"And it's not a publicity stunt?"

"Of course not. Mrs. Christie's a very private person . . . very clever . . . and sensitive."

"And her husband?" There was no reaction. "And what about Nancy Neele, who happens to be on holiday in Harrogate. I gather she's the mistress?"

"That's not true!" said the girl. "Miss Neele's an old friend of the family. She works for the Colonel. No wonder you're a columnist. Despicable lot. Now please leave."

Wally said gently, "You bet she's an old friend. I saw Mrs. Christie at that luncheon and she loves her husband. Her husband's off with that girl and your lady's desperate. Or dead. You really are part of their club, aren't you?"

Charlotte Fisher looked miserable. "I shouldn't have left her that Friday."

"Maybe I can find her."

"If you found her," she said harshly, "you'd write about it."

"Yes, I would. But what are you doing? Listen, in Mrs. Christie's letter to her brother-in-law she said she was going to a Yorkshire spa."

Miss Fisher shook her head. "She canceled Beverley."

"What if she followed Nancy Neele? Went to Harrogate. Then what would she do? Thought of that?"

"She threatened to do something awful in her letter, but the Colonel wouldn't tell me. Won't take her seriously."

"So why haven't you been to the police?"

"Well . . ."

"Because you think Mrs. Christie's done something . . . irregular."

"Don't print that, I beg you."

They were interrupted by the sound of a car pulling into the drive, and the reporter and his unwilling conspirator fell silent.

"You could get out by the back door into the drive," she said.

Wally shook his head. "Going to have to face 'em, Fisher," he said in his best imitation of the English.

Archie Christie was more than astonished to see Miss Fisher, in a dressing gown, come out into the hall followed by a man in a dinner jacket.

"Curious time to entertain, Charlotte. And you've left all the lights on."

"Mr.—"

"I work for Lord Dintworth," Wally said.

"You're Wally Stanton."

"On the nose."

Archie was confused. "Did Harry send you down here?"

"No," Wally said. "But he's on your side."

Archie turned his irritation on the secretary. "I'm afraid Miss Fisher gets a little above herself."

"Not in the least," Wally said. The secretary turned and walked back into the kitchen. Archie stood with his arms folded.

"Rather odd time of the night to come to my house, Mr. Stanton. What can I do for you?"

"Well, Colonel, we have a story coming out tomorrow, and I wanted to make absolutely sure it's accurate, that it represents your point of view."

"Why this time of night?"

"Have to catch the edition, Colonel."

Archie relaxed somewhat. After all, the fellow was influential, he argued to himself, and he came from Dintworth, who was trustworthy. He decided to talk. He led the way into the drawing room.

"I gather your wife may have disappeared voluntarily," Wally said in a concerned sort of voice. "Under stress. In connection with her work, I suppose?" Wally's manner was understanding, trustworthy.

Archie answered. "Yes. I think my wife felt her powers of imagination were failing."

Wally nodded. "I believe Mrs. Christie said she could disappear at will, and of course if she was under stress . . ."

"Exactly so. You can imagine how I feel."

"Pretty embarrassing."

"Indeed," said the Colonel, reassured by Wally's charm. He noted that the journalist's suit came from a good tailor. "Between ourselves, I'm rather displeased with her," he confided. "She overdid this writing business. Made her ill, in my view."

"Well, the best thing would be to find her and shut the whole thing up." Wally paused. "You haven't been giving her shell shock, old man?" he added.

"What!"

"Heard there was a quarrel over a woman."

Christie stood up. "My wife and I had no quarrel," he said coldly. "I've already told the press." He led the way to the front door.

"Oh, good," Wally said as he reached the entrance porch, but the door had already been shut behind him.

He climbed into his car and started the ignition. From the kitchen door, Charlotte Fisher rushed out. Wally rolled down the window, and the girl shoved a folded copy of the *Times* into the car.

"She told me if anything happened to look in the personal column. It could be something to do with her, Mr. Stanton. Can you find out anything from the box number?"

Wally took the newspaper and glanced at the advertisement. "I know a man on the *Times*," he said. "I'll give it a try. You'll have to tell me where Nancy Neele's staying."

"She's at the Valencia Hotel. If you find out anything, please will you let me know?"

Wally thought the secretary looked like a rumpled bird who had lost one of her chicks.

"If it's her, I'll find her."

"Don't you hurt her."

"You're a good girl," he said. Then he drove off.

Chapter 7

Morning sun streamed through the window. Agatha sat at the writing table of her hotel room and read aloud in a neutral voice from a front-page story in the *Post-Despatch*: "My wife and I had no quarrel. There was never any difference of opinion regarding our mutual friends."

She let the newspaper fall to the floor. Her feelings were at once of extreme anger and extreme exultation. She wrote on a piece of paper:

1. To endure loss like a long-term prisoner in the hopes that life will become whole again?
2. Or to take positive action.

It was her habit to force her life into clear-cut alternatives, and that habit remained even in her present state of mind. She wrote down the alternatives as if they were the clues to a crossword puzzle for which there was only one correct solution.

She removed the band from her pack of paper strips. She wrote PLUNGE POOL, PUMP ROOM, MASK, GLOVES, STRAP, RHEOSTAT at the top of separate pieces, then shuffled them together.

The chambermaid, Flora, knocked and came in. "I noticed you've been doing a spot of shopping, ma'am. Wondered if I could help you unpack."

Agatha took pity on the girl's fierce curiosity. "You could take the wrapping off my new table."

Flora jumped at the offer. She made several uncalled-for efforts to tidy the room. "You know this missing novelist, ma'am?" she said, picking up the newspaper from the floor and tapping it. "Mrs. Christie?"

Agatha turned to look at Flora.

"Well, a party of spiritualists is holding a séance around where her car was left."

Agatha's regard was deadpan. "Then they're bound to find her," she said.

Later on that morning Flora spilled out her opinions to her friend, the chef. "I think that Mrs. Neele's run away and likes it!" she said.

The chef shook his head knowingly. "I think she's lost her memory. Doesn't know where her luggage is."

Flora was unconvinced. "Well, she doesn't seem very worried about her luggage. In my view, she's in love. You mark my words, she's come here to meet somebody."

"Curiosity killed the cat," said the chef, wagging his spoon disapprovingly.

"Funny thing about Mrs. Neele," the girl went on.

.The cook stood at the huge hob and stirred several of his iron pots. "Funny what?"

"She doesn't wear a wedding ring," Flora said. "Mind you, Mrs. Neele behaves like a lady."

The lady without the wedding ring was at that moment in the middle of her third treatment with Mrs. Braithwaite. She wore a toweling dressing gown and sat in the Schnee chair with each foot in a cylinder of water and each arm in similar baths attached to the chair's arms. The whole contraption rested on a glass insulating platform. Mrs. Braithwaite switched on the current.

"Now you relax, Mrs. Neele." She sat down by the control panel. "You've certainly got more color than when you arrived. In my view you should get out on the moors and forget about all this treatment. Have you seen Fountains Abbey?"

Agatha shook her head.

"You should. And Haworth. That's where those poor Brontë lasses came from. My older patients don't enjoy it. They say the Brontë parsonage's gloomier than the tomb."

"It sort of tingles," Agatha said.

"That's right, dear."

"It's rather pleasant."

"All of them died."

"What?"

"All of those Brontë girls, as far as I know. Caught cold from damp shoes. Silly bairns."

"Yes, I believe you're right. How does this treatment work?"

"You start slowly, then push up the lever on the shunt rheostat. Very simple, Mrs. Neele. The current goes through the plates in each of those four cylinders."

"And the electrodes are controlled from the panel?"

"That's correct."

Mrs. Braithwaite picked up some knitting. She held up the half-finished waistcoat. "Do you like the pattern?"

"Very nice," Agatha said.

"It's for my son."

"I'm sure he'll be pleased. Yes, this does feel pleasant. What sort of strength am I getting?"

"The handle should be two thirds across the gauge. That's as strong as anyone needs."

"That panel also controls the Galvanic bath, doesn't it?"

"That's right. All the equipment in here is centrally operated. All you have to do is turn on the mains."

"But the Schnee is direct current and the Galvanic is alternating?"

"That's why we use an adapter, but they both come off the same— Goodness me, Mrs. Neele, you'll be doing my job for me."

"Then you can do some more lovely knitting for your son." Agatha smiled.

"I do miss him," the woman said wistfully. "Do you miss your relatives, Mrs. Neele?"

"Oh, very much."

Mrs. Braithwaite looked at the clock. "Two more minutes, dear." She picked up her knitting. "I've another Neele after you, a Miss Nancy Neele. That's a coincidence in the off-season." She got up, pushed down the lever, then turned off the switch. "There you are now. You get dressed and go and rest."

No more than four women occupied the day beds that stretched in long rows under the tiled arches of the Turkish baths. Into the comfortably exotic resting area women came to recover from the rigors of the hot-air baths and the plunge pool.

On adjacent beds lay Agatha and Evelyn, covered by towels. Evelyn was pressing Agatha for a further account of her trip around the world, every detail of which she found of interest. On the subject of South Africa, however, Agatha remained elusive.

"Then did you shoot them?" Evelyn asked.

"No, I'd get a leopard or an elephant in my sights, then call it a day. They didn't approve of me on safari. My husband would say 'Shoot!' and I'd say 'I can't.' It seemed more sporting that way and gave me just as much satisfaction in the end. I knew I wouldn't miss if I actually pulled the trigger. I would think of what my mother always said—that one could carry out anything one set one's mind to."

"Except the kill."

"I loved the sight of those animals more than anything else in the world. I dream about that safari. I suspect I remember it as more exotic than ever it was. Much lusher."

A woman went past them and stopped at a bed several feet away. She took off her gown and carried it across the room to hang it up. Then she got into the bed.

Agatha said, "Have you noticed that a woman, if she's naked, walks on tiptoe?"

Evelyn giggled. "That way, her bosom doesn't wobble."

"Well, I couldn't walk about like that."

"I can't say I'd be bothered." Evelyn raised herself on her elbow. "The first naked body I ever saw was my gran's. I think I must have been about twelve, because we'd just moved to a smaller house and I had to share a bed with her. I remember opening one eye and watching her undress. Torn corsets and old shifts came off and underneath was this shriveled, gallant little body."

"Didn't you have enough to eat?"

"*I* did. I don't know about Gran. She'd worked since she was nine."

"That's awful!"

Evelyn looked at her friend quizzically. "It's not unusual. Our gran gets very angry about things. She's not a frightened person. When the railway men came out last spring in the strike, she was right glad. Went down to the station and told them so. When they all went back to work a few days later, she gave them a piece of her mind."

"Is your grandmother a Communist?" Agatha asked with some alarm.

"Not really." Evelyn laughed. "If you come for Christmas, you'll be quite safe. Bossy she is, but not a Bolshie."

"My grandmother was bossy. Gallant, too, in her way. She was terribly vigilant about men. And I never was."

Evelyn said gently, "You've no guile. You're very clever, Teresa, but you've no guile. If somebody hurt you, you'd show it, and that's the worst thing to do."

Agatha smiled. "You sound like my grandmother. She used to say you should never frighten a man by showing him how much you feel."

"Did you show your feelings?"

Agatha looked away. "Oh, I don't expect so. Grandmother was very Victorian. Like all her generation, she had a lovely time."

"As long as they pretended."

Agatha was no longer attentive. She had seen Nancy Neele enter and had become immediately agitated. She pulled on her robe and held a towel like a hood around her head. Evelyn saw how anguished she looked.

"Is it that cousin of yours?" she asked.

"I'll see you later," Agatha replied.

"Why don't you speak to her?"

"I'd rather not, Evelyn. Not until I'm sure. It might be . . . awkward."

She got up and walked quickly out. She dressed and made her way to the booking desk. The clerk on duty was a woman. "Name please, madam?"

"Neele," Agatha answered.

"Miss Nancy Neele?"

Agatha paused. "Yes. I'd like to check my appointments. Tomorrow at . . . ?"

"Let's see. Tomorrow at two P.M. Tuesday at nine, first appointment."

"Mrs. Braithwaite, as usual?"

"That's right. Room four."

Wally Stanton sat watching her from a table near the desk. He was not entirely sure that the woman in the elegant coat who wore bright-red lipstick was indeed Agatha Christie.

He had traced Mrs. Teresa Neele with ease: his contact at the *Times* had revealed that the advertisement in the personal column came with a Harrogate postmark. And the *Harrogate Herald,* which listed all guests at the spa and named their hotel, told him where the lady was staying. He booked himself a room at the Hydro and signed himself "John Baring, New York City, U.S.A."

The receptionist, the one who in better days had bowed to royalty, did not like Americans. He had heard they were buying up England and over-tipping porters. He read that the Prince of Wales sported an American accent. An American in Harrogate might lead to more Americans coming to the spa, a class of foreign person that would, in his view, disgrace the town. Mr. Baring's luggage was not that of a gentleman, and his friendliness was improper.

Wally glanced through the registry. "See you have a lady all the way from Cape Town."

"We're an international spa," said the receptionist.

"Come all the way from South Africa for treatment?"

"Yes, sir," said the receptionist and snapped the book closed.

"Well, now, what's the form?"

"I beg your pardon?"

"Where do I get treatment?"

"Royal Baths, Mr. Baring. One of the porters will direct you, unless, of course, you require a carriage."

"Just get me a pumpkin," Wally said. "And have my luggage sent up."

A

At the hour when most guests at the Hydro assembled for cards or tea or a sedate afternoon dance, Wally was once more searching for his lady. He found her eventually in the billiards room, where Oscar Jones had persuaded her and Evelyn to join him in a game. To Agatha's dismay, Oscar had also recruited Arthur Benson, the gross guest who continued to show disturbing interest in Mrs. Teresa Neele.

The game was already in progress when Wally walked in. He sat down next to Uncle Jones, who was watching the play from his wheelchair, and looked around the paneled room with its little brass Victorian lamps, green baize table, and walls lined with cue racks.

The lady for whom a whole country searched had chosen the company of a blubber-faced young man who wore sandals, a pretty woman with a north-country accent, and a middle-aged man with an Edwardian moustache. Wally noted the pleated silk dress, which barely reached Agatha's knee, her elegant hair style. Her smile said she had not a care in the world. He took a deep breath, lit a cigarette, and wiped his speculative palette clean. If he could no longer follow the scenario, he was at least a member of the audience.

Evelyn deftly handled her cue and cannoned the red off the cushion into the middle pocket. Agatha responded with a mock groan of disappointment.

"Jolly good," said Oscar, smiling his eager, deranged-looking smile. He hitched up the blanket over his uncle's knees, then stood back with Agatha while Benson took his shot. Wally came up alongside them as if to better observe the play.

"Takes forever, doesn't he?" Oscar said. "You know, Mrs. Neele, you look rather like that woman who disappeared."

Agatha continued to watch the game.

"Yes, indeed. Mrs. Christie," Oscar continued. "Pretty woman. Read any of her stuff?"

"That was a poor shot," Agatha said. She turned toward Oscar. "Yes, I have, as a matter of fact."

"*The Murder of Roger Ackroyd,* did you read it?" Oscar threw up his arms. "That was cunning. Do you think she cheated?"

"No, Mr. Jones. If you read the book carefully, you'll find you're wrong. My turn." Agatha picked up her cue and began to line up a shot. Benson came up from behind, leaned over her to adjust the angle of the cue, leaned a little too long and too close. Quite suddenly Agatha began to panic, unable to deal with the familiarity, seemingly unable either to go on playing or move away.

Wally reached for a piece of chalk, stood with his back to the table, and politely removed Oscar Jones's cue from the boy's hand. He began to chalk the end while managing at the same time to lunge the stick backward into Benson. The man released his hold on Agatha and spun around.

"What the devil!"

"Terribly sorry." Wally grinned. He handed the cue back to Oscar. "That should be better." Then he dropped the chalk.

He bent down to look for it, and Agatha, released from her captor, knelt down to join the search. It was a way of covering her distress.

From his crouched position Wally looked up at her and smiled. "Shall we dance?"

She looked at the stranger, then she got up. Wally stood alongside her. She was several inches taller than he. "On second thought," he said, "perhaps I'm not up to it."

She smiled and said, "I insist."

Wally turned to the rest of the group and held up the piece of chalk like a trophy. "My apologies for the interruption. John Baring. How do you do?"

Oscar came forward to shake the newcomer's hand. "Jolly good of you to chalk my cue."

"Don't mention it."

Wally turned to Benson. "Hope I didn't hurt you."

"Yes, you did. I must say, you might have been more careful."

"Mr. Benson," Evelyn said, "I think that's rather unfriendly of you. As far as I'm concerned, the game's at an end. You've really ruined it for me and I think you should apologize to Mr. . . . Baring."

This piece of playacting had its effect. Benson mumbled a surly apology and left the room.

Evelyn whistled and raised her arms. "Got rid of him! Well done, Mr. Baring. I'm Evelyn Crawley. This is Mrs. Neele, and this is Oscar Jones. And that"—she indicated the comatose man in the wheelchair—"may well still be Mr. Jones's uncle."

Everybody laughed.

"I think you saved me from a fate worse than death," Agatha said.

"Then it was worth it." Wally smiled.

"Have you just arrived?"

Wally nodded. There was a small silence.

"All the way from America?" Agatha asked.

"Not exactly. I'm in the textile business. Brings me up here once a year. Thought I'd"—he looked earnestly around the group—"dry out."

To cover what she presumed to be an embarrassing confession, Agatha said brightly, "Evelyn's in textiles, in Bradford."

"Oh, really?" Wally said. "And where do you come from, Mrs. Neele?"

"From South Africa."

"One of my favorite places. Cape Town?"

"Yes," she answered in a way that warned him off further questions.

He didn't care to lose his advantage. "Look, I'm just arrived, on my own, and I'm a little bit lost. Could I possibly persuade you people to join me for dinner?"

Wally sat between Agatha and Evelyn in the almost empty dining room. Oscar Jones had kept the table unamused well into the fish course with an analysis of *Patience,* his favorite Gilbert and Sullivan opera. Wally was making no progress. He watched Agatha as closely as he could. She wore a velvet dinner dress, which showed off her handsome shoulders, and a rope of pearls. He wondered whether her remarkable change of appearance and apparent good spirits indicated a personality change or even a genuine loss of memory. And how and where had she procured the funds to dress so expensively? Colonel Christie had told the police that neither of their joint bank accounts had been drawn upon since his wife's disappearance, and she was said to have left home with not much more than five pounds.

When Uncle Jones woke up, began to pound the sides of his chair, and to complain he'd missed out on the soup, Wally was able to gain Agatha's attention.

"Will you be staying for long?"

"I suppose until my cure is completed," she answered.

He nodded.

"What kind of textiles are you in, Mr. Baring?"

He smiled broadly. "Very polite of you to ask, but I'm not going to bore you with the answer. At heart I'm more of a writer than a businessman. Amateur, of course."

"A writer," she said, with interest. "What do you write?"

"Fiction. It's tidier than fact."

Agatha nodded enthusiastically. "And you can do what you like with your characters, isn't that so?"

Evelyn interrupted. "What sort of fiction, Mr. Baring?"

"Mostly short stories."

"Have you published anything?" Agatha pursued.

"One or two things in small magazines. Thought

I might try something while I'm up here. Look, you people can help. I found this today in the *Times* personal column. Went like this: 'Ethel come home. This time as housekeeper. Lamp incident forgotten.'" He noted how attentively Agatha listened.

"I think that's a short story in itself," he continued.

"Lonely woman?" Evelyn suggested.

Agatha began to tap the ends of her fingers on the table. "Bachelor in love with his maid? Peculiar husband? I love puzzles."

"A murder trap, perhaps," Wally suggested.

"Possibly," Agatha answered. "Puzzling more than gruesome, I should say, like all good detective fiction."

"You know, I think you're absolutely right."

"Try a trick," she continued. "Great fun."

"Yes, that's true, but an advertisement like that makes you want to find out the truth. Truth's undoubtedly stranger than fiction, though I know that's a cliché."

Evelyn interrupted. "Better than your advertisement in the *Times*, Teresa."

"Yes," she answered, all enthusiasm vanished.

"Mrs. Neele's looking for her relatives," Evelyn explained.

"Found one?" Wally asked.

"Not yet."

The table fell silent, so that Uncle Jones could be heard sucking the remains of his pudding off the spoon.

"May I offer you all some coffee?" Wally asked.

"Won't serve it in here," Uncle Jones said. "They like to keep you moving."

"Well, then, shall we move?"

"I think, if you'll forgive me, I'll go to bed," Agatha said.

"But you promised me a dance."

"I don't dance."

He smiled. "But I do."

"So do I," Evelyn said. "And so does Oscar. He wants to dance professionally."

Oscar looked bashful and nodded.

"Over my dead body," said Uncle Jones.

Wally stood up. "Then, Mrs. Neele, I suggest that you and I and Mr. Jones watch the performance."

The group moved off to the ballroom and occupied a table close to the dance floor. Two elderly couples were dancing a slow foxtrot to the music of Harry Codd's band. When the leader changed to a tango, Oscar invited Evelyn onto the floor. In no time he was swooping and bending his partner across the floor in his own unorthodox version of the dance.

"That boy's an exhibitionist," complained Uncle Jones.

"Nonsense," said Agatha patting the old man. "He's very stylish."

"All he wants to do is sing and dance. It's my belief he gets it from his mother. Girl had bad blood. My brother should never have married her. Hopeless in the business he was, and all because of that woman. Took to the bottle and left—that!" Uncle Jones lifted his arm to indicate his nephew.

He paused dramatically. "Left that big lummock to me."

"Oscar's not a lummock,"Agatha said, catching Wally's eye.

"Oscar's himself," Wally added.

"Exactly."

"He certainly doesn't care for ball bearings!" roared Uncle Jones. "Who's going to take care of them when I'm gone?"

Agatha reached into Evelyn's bag and took out the brandy flask. She poured some surreptitiously into Uncle Jones's coffee cup and offered it to Wally.

"Mrs. Neele," he said, "you're the nicest thief I ever met. I come here to dry out and you offer me brandy."

"I'm frightfully sorry," she said. "I should have remembered."

"Actually, I'm not a drunk or anything. I've just had a very painful time recently and sort of taken to the bottle."

"I'm so sorry."

"My fiancée walked out on me." He shook his head. "I'm afraid we Americans always tell all. And that can be awfully boring."

"It's not the least boring." She leaned forward. "Can't you get her back?"

"I don't think so. I don't think she loves me." He paused. "Would you stay with someone who didn't love you?"

"That depends," she said.

"But then I presume you're very much loved."

"My husband died recently."

"I'm really sorry."

Agatha picked up her shawl. She turned to Uncle Jones to change the subject. "He's asleep. I can't imagine Oscar going into ball bearings, can you? Look at him."

Oscar had persuaded Harry Codd and his men to try a Charleston. He was now master of the floor. His legs splayed out all over the place, as if made of rubber, in a frenzy of effortful pleasure. Next to him Evelyn's neat legs flashed out like matches against tinder.

"Come on, let's give them some competition."

"I can't, Mr. Baring. I'm no good."

"Well, I'm a champ. You follow me."

He took her hand and led her onto the floor.

"I could never learn to dance properly," she shouted over the music. "Always too worried about what to say."

"Well, you sure as heck don't have to talk to me," he shouted back. "I *need* my breath."

"My legs aren't right," she said. "I think they're too long."

"They're beautiful."

"They won't bend properly."

He could see that, as the music got faster, Agatha found it more difficult to keep pace and that her expression of gaiety became frenetic. He had the feeling that, knowingly or unknowingly, she had extended the boundary of her disguise. He saw the same look on her face he had registered at the literary lunch. Now he had her trapped, and he kept her dancing.

The unexpected pleasure she felt in the company of this newcomer served to remind her of past happiness, of good times, and of Archie. Out of an unbearable crisis of feeling, she had escaped to an unreal order of her own invention. Her enjoyment of the evening had upset this curious equilibrium. She had unguardedly abandoned the habit of pain and knew it to be a betrayal.

The harder she tried to keep up with the steps the more her body refused instruction.

John Baring became Archie, Archie in uniform pacing around her like a circus master, telling her how to move, not to make a fool of herself. The room began to spin and blur till all Agatha registered was her husband's demonic smile and his arm signaling the beat. Then she blacked out and fell.

When she regained consciousness, she found herself lying on the empty dance floor, her head supported by Evelyn, while Wally Stanton held a glass of brandy to her lips. She looked confused and frightened.

"You fainted," Evelyn said. "Drink the brandy." Agatha looked around her, at Oscar Jones standing gawping, at the silent musicians, and at the staring elderly guests.

"I'm so sorry," she said to Wally. "I'm an awfully dangerous dancing partner."

"But terrific." He smiled at her.

Wally and Evelyn helped her to a chair while Oscar lunged from one foot to another as if to clear a way.

"I hope Harrogate has a cure for the Charleston," he ventured.

"Harrogate never heard of the Charleston till

tonight," Wally said. He lifted the brandy glass. "Go on, Mrs. Neele. Drink up or you won't get the next dance."

When Agatha felt strong enough to stand, Evelyn helped her to her room.

Wally walked slowly through the Winter Garden smoking a cigarette. He felt his hunch had proved correct. What was it the old woman had said to him in the pub? "And then his glasses broke and I couldn't see him." That was what old Violet had said. Her "other self" dreamed of a dancing partner. Like Violet, Agatha Christie had invented another life to deal with the pain of her own. Like Violet, she did not quite trust in this invention. The poor, toothless spinster and the privileged author from the upper class shared a blinding lack of self-confidence.

Wally went to telephone his secretary. He woke the girl up. "Polly, I've found her. And you've got to help."

"Where are you?"

"Harrogate. I want you to find the best doctor you can and ask him how amnesiacs behave. I want to know why the hell Mrs. Christie's taken the mistress's name."

"What about your column, Wally?"

"You're going to write it."

"I can't do that."

"Yes, you can. There's enough material lying about on my desk. You glue it together. Prince of Wales learning the Charleston at the Café de Paris. That story about Americans invading the hunting field. Head it 'The New Vandals.' And the stuff about them buying up castles and overtipping rustics. Nothing those readers like better than a good sneer. Start with my interview with H. G. Wells."

"You've already used it."

"There's more good things in my notes."

"How about that photograph of Dame Nellie Melba? That'll overexcite them, of course."

"Polly, my name's John Baring. Try and telephone Harrogate 405 tomorrow with the dope on amnesia. Keep it under your hat and call me tomorrow. I kiss you."

Evelyn helped Agatha to bed. She ordered some broth from the kitchen and sat by her friend while she spooned it up.

"I can't imagine why I fainted."

"Teresa, how long ago did your husband die?"

Agatha paused. "It was six months ago."

"Well, in my view you're trying to stifle your grief, probably more than you ought. People do that, you know, when they feel very deeply."

"I suppose that's very interfering." Evelyn took her friend's hand. "But you're a special sort of woman."

Agatha shook her head. "I'm very ordinary."

"Perhaps you're both. You're certainly clever and curious and attractive. And all sorts of other things. It's just awfully unfair that you aren't happy."

"The trouble is," Agatha said, "I always expected to be."

Evelyn smiled. "I never expected it."

"Stay for another minute."

Evelyn took away the soup bowl.

"One has to put things right," Agatha said. "Evelyn, would you help me?"

"Of course I will."

"I've got to go to Leeds tomorrow to find out about my luggage. Well, I've found out that woman who I think is my cousin is called Neele. The one I pointed out at the baths. The clerk told me her name. Don't you think that's remarkable? It's got to be Nancy."

"Have you tried to contact her?"

"Well, no . . . What if she isn't . . . my cousin?"

"I'm sure she wouldn't mind if you tried to find out."

Agatha paused.

"Evelyn, she has her appointment tomorrow afternoon at two. Now, as you have to be there, couldn't you possibly . . . approach her? Find out if she comes from Rickmansworth."

"If you'd really like me to."

"I really would."

"Well, then, of course."

Evelyn could see that her friend seemed very relieved. So much so that, shortly after, she fell asleep.

Evelyn picked up the book on hydrotherapy that was lying on the sidetable and thumbed through it. A piece of paper fell out from the pages. She picked it up. In Agatha's handwriting were the following words:

> All my life
> Dream-haunted by loss

Till you
When I didn't dream
But closed my eyes.
Now alone
I am pursued again.

Evelyn put the poem back in the book and crept out of the room.

Chapter 8

Wally Stanton sat in the small lobby of the Valencia Hotel. It was seven o'clock on a bone-cold morning, and he couldn't make up his mind whether to spill the beans or sit on the Christie story till he could make more sense of it. Wally knew that his own motives for pursuing the story were mixed. Partly, he wanted the satisfaction of being first, and of telling a story, for a change, "straight and true," as he had been trained to do. Partly, he wanted revenge on Dintworth and Archie Christie and their kind. They represented the entrenched privileged that had forced his own parents, poor industrial workers, to emigrate. Wally had come back to England only to discover that Dintworth and company not only controlled the economy, but also wielded the political power. The system had victimized him in a small way, as it had to a larger extent his parents. These thoughts were interrupted by the head porter of the Valencia Hotel. He nudged Wally's arm. "That's her, sir."

Wally saw a pretty dark-haired girl, accompanied by an elderly woman, cross the vestibule toward the exit. He tipped the porter generously and followed Nancy Neele down the steps to the street. The doorman summoned a taxi and told the cabbie to take the ladies to the Royal Pump Room. Wally followed.

At that hour of the morning it was customary for the streets around the Pump Room to be roped off for the benefit of morning visitors who came to drink a pint or two of sulphur water and to follow that routine with a good walk. Wally's cab was forced to pull up at some distance from the Pump Room, and by the time he reached the entrance he had lost Nancy Neele. He was about to enter the building when he saw Agatha standing some feet away. She wore a cloche hat pulled well down over her face and a fur coat with a high collar.

"Morning, Mrs. Neele. Hope you're feeling better."

"I'm much better," she said.

"You're certainly muffled up this morning. Recognized your legs, as a matter of fact. Otherwise, I might have missed you. Never forget a dancing partner's legs."

She smiled slightly. He noticed that her eyes flicked back and forth to the entrance of the Pump Room.

"Mrs. Neele, would you share my morning's dose of poison?"

"I don't think I want to take the waters today."

"Great for the eyesight."

She shook her head.

"Come on, you mean you haven't got the nerve to go in."

Agatha said, "I really loathe the taste."

"Look," he said, "I've promised my therapist I'll take this stuff, and I need your encouragement. Otherwise, it's back to Miss Crawley's brandy flask."

He took her arm gently and they walked into the hall that led down to the drinking fountain. His companion was noticeably agitated. Fifty feet away, Nancy Neele and her aunt stood holding the small cups of water. Wally saw that Agatha could not take her eyes off the women. He bought a guide book at the entrance and began to read from it. "Cupola's early Victorian. Shall we go have a closer look? Man called William Slingsby found a sulphur well here around 1570."

"Do you mind if we sit down for a moment?" Agatha asked. "I'm still feeling rather weak."

"Of course not. Know what they used to call Harrogate? The 'stinking spa.' Fifteen hundred suckers drank the stinking stuff one morning last summer. Anything else you want to know?"

Agatha was staring at Nancy Neele.

"Come on, let's be brave."

His companion refused to move.

"Now that girl in the dark-blue coat. She's actually smiling, Mrs. Neele. So the water can't be that bad."

"She's very pretty, don't you think?"

"Pretty? I wouldn't say so. Rather ordinary,

really. Very bland. I know it's impertinent of me to say so, but you have a beautiful face and that girl is, well, simply forgettable."

"To me she looks very attractive."

"Okay, Mrs. Neele. I'll prove you're wrong. If we walk over there and eavesdrop . . ."

Agatha looked at her watch. "I'm so sorry, but I have to go." She got up and almost ran out of the building.

Wally went after her. He saw her turn up Crescent Road and followed her. He had almost to run to keep pace. Halfway up King's Road she stopped and went into a hardware shop. She seemed to be on a purposeful journey and he decided not to interrupt her. He stood for a while outside the shop, peering through the bow window. He saw Agatha take out a piece of paper and show it to the assistant. There was some conversation between them while the man examined the piece of paper. He fetched some wire, a screwdriver, and a rheostat, and began to work at it, all the time demonstrating what he was doing and referring to the piece of paper. Then he wrapped up various articles, and Agatha paid and left.

As she came out of the shop, Wally stopped her. "Mrs. Neele, I lost you."

She said coldly, "Mr. Baring, I lost you."

He saw how drawn she looked, how little she welcomed his reappearance.

"I'm terribly sorry. It's true, I did follow you. I haven't followed a girl like this since . . . It's ridiculous."

"Yes, it is," she said. "Probably because Harrogate's such a boring place, Mr. Baring."

"Do you think so?"

"I'm sure Evelyn Crawley would be delighted to keep you company. She's awfully agreeable. And I'm not."

"I beg to differ. It's not just because you've such a lovely face," he said. "I like your company." He was walking beside her along the road. "There's something very intimate about friendship with a stranger."

"I'm afraid I don't agree."

Wally Stanton was defeated. He lifted his hat and smiled at her. "Then I shall say good morning and leave you be."

He turned and walked away. He went down the street to the public telephone booth and dialed the number of the *Globe-Enquirer*. When he got through to his office, he asked to speak to Polly.

"What d'ya find out?"

"Are you still in Harro—?"

"Yes, and don't say where, in case somebody's listening in. What did you find out, Polly?"

"I spoke to two specialists. Said I had a friend suffering from amnesia and that she'd taken on somebody else's name. Both of them gave me the same answer. They said that a true amnesiac is too desperately busy trying to remember his own name to take on somebody else's."

Wally let out a low whistle.

"Maybe it's just very simple: she wants to be the mistress."

"Perhaps," Wally said. There was a long silence.

"Wally, are you still there?"

"Yes, I'm here."

"I wrote your column for you. Said you'd done it from your sickbed."

"Polly, you're an angel. You know, the same thing happened to me when I was a young reporter on the *Denver Post*. One of our best men disappeared, so I wrote his piece. Know what they did? They gave me his job, and when he showed up they fired him."

Polly laughed. "Only I used your stuff," she said. "I just corrected the spelling. By the way, a woman keeps on calling for you. She sounds a bit agitated. Won't give her name, says to ask you if you've found the advertisement."

"Uh huh. When she telephones again, tell her not to worry. And tell Briggs I'm not sick and not in bed and that I've found Mrs. Christie, but say you don't know where I am. Tell him to get to work on Dintworth. I want a promise in writing he'll print my story. Otherwise . . ."

"Otherwise what?"

"I dunno. I don't know whether she's nuts or not, but I think she's up to something."

A week had passed since his wife had disappeared, and Archibald Christie was showing signs of extreme strain. His wife's disappearance had profoundly damaged his sense of himself. He had no practice in dealing with the scandal. The very unordinariness of his situation frightened him. Finally, he was intimidated by the publicity. He even doubted his own version of his wife's disappearance. The promise of Nancy Neele and of a future happiness seemed remote, if not improbable. In the early evening of the Saturday after his wife's disappearance, he paced their bedroom while Charlotte Fisher searched through the wardrobe.

"Agatha's never owned a green dress," he said.

"They think this woman in Kensington looked like Agatha," Miss Fisher explained. "And I promised we'd go through everything to make sure nothing is missing."

"Which woman in Kensington, Charlotte? The country's full of women masquerading as my wife. One in Torquay, dozens in London, and half of sodding Sunningdale." He paced about. "I can't stand it."

Charlotte Fisher pulled out a dress and showed it to Archie. She said in a neutral voice, "This one's green."

Archie collapsed into a chair. "It's so shaming. You know, if there hadn't been this publicity . . . She must know what it's doing to me."

"She liked publicity even less than you."

"What do you mean 'liked.' You make it sound as if she's dead. You know perfectly well that's not true."

"How should I know, Colonel?" The girl's pudding face looked angry. "If you drive someone enough, who knows what they'll do."

Agatha walked along the low-ceilinged corridor past several therapy rooms. She opened a door

marked "Private," saw that the room appeared to
be empty, and entered. She was in the therapists'
changing room: day clothes hung on several
hooks. There were washbasins, mirrors, a chaise
longue, and one or two armchairs. Pinned to the
wall was a large timetable laying out the therapists' appointments for the month. Agatha studied
the timetable carefully, noting Mrs. Braithwaite's
telephone number. She ran her finger down the
therapist's list of patients, found her own and
Nancy Neele's appointments. She saw that many
times remained blank, because of the season, and
she checked which therapy rooms would be empty
that afternoon.

Then the door opened and a uniformed therapist walked in. Agatha moved awkwardly to the
center of the room.

"I think I've come to the wrong place," she
said.

"Well, yes, madam. This room's private. May
I help you?"

Agatha apologized and walked hastily out.

She went back along the corridor to Therapy
Room 3. She checked her watch, made sure that
nobody saw her, and then went in by way of the
consulting room.

Once inside, she examined the place carefully.
She saw that the equipment was almost identical
to that in Mrs. Braithwaite's therapy room, and
that each mode of treatment was wired to one
wall panel. She looked at her watch once again
and checked that the two other rooms which made
up the therapy suite were empty. She opened the
hand valise she was carrying and went to work

on the panel. With the aid of a diagram, she unscrewed the rheostat and changed the wires from one terminal to another. She switched on the current, pushed up the lever, and noted the reading on the clock. Then she rearranged the wires. She put a length of electrical cord and her screwdriver back into her case, and left.

Agatha opened the door to Therapy Room 4 and looked around to make sure there was no one in the suite of rooms. She put a note in block letters on Mrs. Braithwaite's desk. It read: MISS NEELE HAS HAD TO CANCEL HER APPOINTMENT FOR 2:00 P.M.

Wally was in luck. He found Nancy Neele sitting at one of the small wicker tables in the entrance hall of the Royal Baths. Also at the table was an elderly woman, holding in one hand a hearing-aid and in the other a walking stick. More old people occupied nearby tables, and in one corner of the room a pianist played the tune of "If These Lips Could Only Speak." Wally sang the words to himself as he crossed the room, limping ostentatiously. He winced with particular zeal as he reached Nancy's table and leaned on the back of an unoccupied chair.

"Would you mind terribly if I sat down for a minute?"

"Of course not," Nancy said.

"I've a gammy leg. Old war wound."

Nancy gave him a smile of polite concern.

"Good afternoon," he addressed their table companion, who made no reply.

"She's deaf," Nancy whispered, "and dumb, I believe."

"That's why the pianist is playing 'If These Lips Could Only Speak.'"

Nancy laughed. "I hope you're getting the proper treatment for that leg." The girl was civil and unflirtatious. Wally noticed the dark lines under her eyes. He thought she looked as if she'd held her breath for too long, waiting for an answer to her life. Her skin and eyes looked lifeless.

"Do you come to Harrogate often?" Wally asked.

"No," she said. "This is the first time." She obviously had no mind to continue the conversation.

After a pause Wally leaned toward her. He said earnestly, "I know you're not supposed to make personal remarks in this country, but I'm an American and I just have to speak my mind."

"Oh, yes?"

"You're really pretty. I'd like to add that I'm madly in love with my wife, so I can't flirt with you."

Nancy looked embarrassed. "You came all the way from America for your leg?"

"Yep. Only place in the world where I can get satisfaction."

"How extraordinary," the girl answered.

"Isn't it? My wife hates the place."

"Well, it's not much fun."

"Can't imagine why *you'd* come here."

She blushed a little. "To tell you the truth, I've come to lose weight."

Wally wrinkled his brow. "First, I'd like to say that's unnecessary. Second, why are you here on your own?"

Nancy was pleased to have somebody to talk to. "My fiancé was going to join me," she said, "but he's been held up."

"When's the wedding?"

"Tomorrow, if I had my way."

"I bet he feels the same way as you do."

"Oh, yes. Yes, he does, as a matter of fact." Her smile faded.

Wally looked concerned. "No problems, I hope?"

"Oh, no."

"Well, I'd really be flattered if you'd have tea with me one day. I think that's the appropriate meal for you and me in our circumstances. My name's John Baring."

He made a painful-looking effort to rise, and in so doing noticed Evelyn Crawley coming across to the table accompanied by the male clerk.

The clerk addressed Miss Neele. "This lady would like to speak to you."

Wally pulled up another chair to the table. He noted that Evelyn Crawley was as agitated as he was curious. She nodded to Wally and then turned to Nancy.

"My name's Evelyn Crawley. Do forgive me for approaching you but I've a friend here, a Mrs. Teresa Neele from South Africa." She paused for a moment and then decided to continue despite Wally's presence. "She's a friend of Mr. Baring's, too. You see, your name's spelt the same way."

"Yes?" Nancy said.

"She's come back to try and trace her relatives. Well, she heard the clerk mention your name, found out you'd be here today—"

Wally interrupted. "Why isn't Teresa here herself?"

"She went to Leeds this afternoon," Evelyn explained. "To see about her lost luggage. Asked me to meet you and . . . Do you know, I find this all rather difficult."

"You'd like Mrs. Neele," Wally said.

"Well, I'm sure." The girl sounded uncertain.

"She saw you in the Turkish baths," Evelyn went on. "She's convinced you're her cousin from Rickmansworth."

"I do live there," Nancy said, cagily. "But I don't think we have any relatives in South Africa."

"Very strange," Wally said.

"My friend's awfully shy," Evelyn continued. "She wanted me to make the approach."

"Teresa's not the least bit shy," Wally said.

Nancy stood up. "I'm afraid I have to go to my appointment now. Thank you for passing on the message. But please tell your friend I very much doubt that we're related."

She shook Wally's hand. "I do hope your leg improves."

She said her good-byes and walked away.

"I didn't know you had a bad leg," Evelyn said.

"And Miss Neele doesn't know this cousin."

"I simply can't understand why Teresa's so obsessed with her relatives," Evelyn complained.

"Perhaps she's lonely?"

"Yes. Her husband died recently. And . . . she's such a nice woman but she's . . ."

"Heading for a nervous breakdown, perhaps?"

"Perhaps," Evelyn answered and got up to go. She had the strongest feeling she might have betrayed her friend's confidence.

Agatha looked at her watch and then locked the door of Therapy Room 3. She changed rapidly. She put on a white therapist's gown over her wool dress, tied her hair in a black net, and fixed a surgical mask across her face. She left her coat and case under the desk in the consulting room and walked out into the hall.

Two patients passed her. Agatha stood in an alcove of the stone-vaulted hall with her back half turned to passers-by. She held some papers close to her face. Ten minutes passed, then Mrs. Braithwaite turned down the corridor from the direction of the therapists' changing room. She opened the door of Therapy Room 4 in order to keep her first appointment of the afternoon. A minute later Nancy Neele entered the corridor from the opposite direction. Agatha guessed that Mrs. Braithwaite, having found the note canceling her appointment, would consult the clerk. It was touch and go how long she would remain in the room.

As Nancy Neele made to enter Therapy Room 4, Agatha stopped her.

"Miss Neele?"

"That's right."

Agatha lowered her voice and copied Evelyn's north-country accent. "This way, my dear."

"But I've an appointment with Mrs. Braithwaite."

"I know, Miss Neele. Poor Jessica's come down with the flu and I'm to look after you. This way, please."

Nancy followed the woman into Therapy Room 3. Agatha sat down behind the desk and opened a file. "Let's see, you've had the . . ."

"Steam treatment," Nancy said.

"That's right. How much have you lost?"

"Five pounds."

"That's good. Today we'll try you on the Galvanic bath."

Nancy looked unhappy. "I'm not ill. I mean, you don't have to wear a surgical mask."

"Oh, yes I do, Miss Neele. I've had this awful flu myself. But I'm on the mend. Of course, Mrs. Braithwaite has to be extra careful. She's getting on, you know." She closed the file. "Now, you go and change."

Nancy Neele went into the adjoining room while Agatha ran warm water into the bath. She checked the panel with shaking hands.

When Nancy returned, wearing a toweling robe, the new therapist showed her the control panel. "It's quite simple. I turn this lever to the required level. Then I switch on. Here."

Nancy looked over her shoulder at the maze of pipes and wiring.

"Goodness me, you're not to worry. It won't hurt you. You'll just feel a pleasant tingling. Tighten those muscles!"

Nancy looked back at the panel.

"All I do is switch it on," Agatha said. "Now,

in you get. We'll start very gently." She turned on the current.

"Here for long, Miss Neele?"

"Another week I think."

"With a friend?"

"With my aunt, as a matter of fact."

"A pretty girl like you not married?"

Nancy relaxed a little and settled back in the warm water. "Engaged, as a matter of fact— I'm sorry, I don't know your name."

"Miss Horton," Agatha said. She remained standing at the instrument panel.

Nancy said in a friendly way, "You're not married either, then?"

"Can't say I wish to be" came the reply. "Too much encroachment," she added, using a phrase of Evelyn's.

"I can barely feel a thing, Miss Horton."

"Then I'll turn it up a little."

Before she could do so they were interrupted. A woman put her head around the therapy-room door.

"Oh, excuse me," she said. "I was looking for Miss Allen."

"Are you sure your appointment's for today?"

"Well, I think so," the woman said.

Agatha turned off the switch and told Nancy to get dressed. "We'll carry on next week."

She asked the woman to wait, and handed Nancy a towel. "Change as fast as you can. We're behind schedule."

Agatha went into the consulting room, picked up her case and coat, and walked out. She crossed the corridor to a lavatory, where she removed net, mask and uniform, and put them into her bag.

⋀

When Wally returned to the Hydro from the Royal Baths, he asked the hotel porter for a list of shipping companies to find out which of them worked the route between Cape Town and Britain.

"You know that Mrs. Neele has lost her luggage. Well, I'd like to help her," he said. "Frankly, I don't think she's having much success in finding it. Needs a little assistance. But keep it under your cap," he added. "She might be offended if she thought I was interfering."

The porter nodded knowingly.

"Now, if you can discover which line Mrs. Teresa Neele used, then get through to the right branch in Leeds—that's where she expects her luggage to be delivered."

"I'll make a thorough investigation, sir," the porter said, picking up the tip he was offered with practiced discretion.

Wally went up to his room on the second floor. He poured some whiskey into a glass. It was not his custom to drink during the afternoon, but he was more depressed than he normally allowed himself to be. He had put his job at risk, propelled by an angry whim. Though he had found the lady for whom the rest of the country was searching—something of a coup in itself—he had not discovered what the lady was up to; did her behavior the last few days suggest some sinister plan? There was less than a week's grace before his next Sunday column was due to be delivered.

Wally sipped his whiskey and weighed the advantages of breaking the story immediately against waiting till he could find out more about Mrs. Christie's plan. But what if she had no plan? There was the further possibility that at any minute somebody else would recognize her. Wally worked over the case: Agatha Christie had followed her husband's mistress to Harrogate and taken on Nancy Neele's surname. The obvious, simple explanation was that she wished to identify with the woman loved by Archie Christie.

But he was still not entirely sure whether the novelist's radically altered mode of dress and make-up was an effort to copy the more youthful Nancy Neele, or had been contrived as a deliberate disguise. Whatever the explanation, Mrs. Christie seemed surprisingly unconcerned about public recognition. Perhaps she felt that her changed appearance, and the privacy of a spa town out of season, ensured her safety. Or was she too obsessed with her private drama to care about the outside world? Wally reminded himself how coolly she had handled Oscar Jones; when during the billiards game, the boy had told her she resembled the missing novelist, she had seemed unperturbed. She had even defended her own book in the manner of somebody enjoying a private joke or an elaborate trick. That reaction, and the information Polly had given him about amnesiac behavior, destroyed the loss-of-memory theory. And yet . . .

Wally helped himself to more whiskey and sat back on the narrow bed. Although she might be a confidence trickster, she was also in pain. She was the kind of woman who invited pain; he had sensed that the first time he saw her. She had the innocence and the arrogance to presume on a continuous present.

He began to look into the corners of his own life. He had worked hard, he could please while giving the impression of being his own man. He could afford to take lightly what he wrote about because he so rarely exposed his opinions. His readers thought that stylish; he knew his jesting was often craven. In his private life Wally had never loved a girl deeply enough to get hurt. That conclusion, by no means new to him, suddenly seemed revealing. He wasn't, after all, running after the lady to spite the ruling class or to take a risk for a change, but rather to find out about a woman who had made an emotional commitment of which he was incapable. . . .

He got up and ran a bath. He lay back in the warm water with his glass of whiskey on a chair within reach. "It's not that simple," he said aloud. He was back grappling with the riddles. Agatha Christie was hardly superficial. The personality that emerged from her books was earthbound, practical, watchful, and humorous. Above all, she was a guileful writer. She formulated complicated plots like algebraic puzzles.

Whatever her present condition, she constantly confounded him: he had seen her capacity for pleasure, along with a pain so sharp she had blocked it out by fainting.

He changed for dinner and brushed his thick brown hair neatly into place. What were the threats Agatha had made, that Charlotte Fisher had told him about, the threats that Archie Christie wouldn't take seriously? He filled his silver cigarette case slowly and checked that his lighter was in place. The chambermaid knocked and asked if she could prepare the room for the night. He was about to tell her to come back later when an idea occurred to him. He smiled at the young Yorkshire girl and asked her name.

"Mary, sir," she said, surprised. It wasn't customary for gentlemen to ask your name.

"Well," he said, "I wonder if you'd be kind enough to help me. There's a very charming woman staying here called Mrs. Neele. Do you know the lady?"

"The one without any luggage?"

"That's right."

"Yes, I do. But she's not on my floor."

"Who looks after her?"

"Flora, sir. Flora thinks she's here because of a gentleman. I told her it was none of her . . ." The girl suddenly looked at him and blushed.

Wally guessed what she was thinking. He simulated mild embarrassment. "The thing is, I'd very much like you to persuade Flora to leave a little gift in Mrs. Neele's room." He lowered his voice dramatically. "Couldn't possibly send it up with the porter. Might cause . . . talk. It's a very private matter."

The girl nodded.

"May I ask if you've ever been in love?"

"Yes, sir. I have."

"Well, in that case you'll understand." Wally looked his most earnest. "Any chance of your finding Flora for me? If I could speak to her in private . . ."

"No problem, sir. But she's very . . . I mean, she's not one to hold her tongue."

"I quite understand. But she could be helpful to me. And as long as my secret remains with you, may I count on your discretion?"

"You may," she said.

A few minutes later the maid came running back to Wally's room with Flora in tow.

Wally winked conspiratorially at Mary and whispered, "I'll speak to you later." Then he shut the door gently on the disappointed girl and turned to Flora. She was not pretty, but he liked her sharp little face. Her neat body expressed a restless energy barely tapped in her life as a chambermaid. Wally knew at once that he could use her. He looked at the girl and sighed.

"Yes, sir?" she asked impatiently.

"I'm not sure I have any right to ask your help. You see, it's a very private matter, Miss . . . ?"

"Flora, sir."

"On the other hand, you're the only person who can help me."

"Well, what is it then?"

"Not even Mary must know."

"Oh, I wouldn't tell a soul. It concerns Mrs. Neele, doesn't it?"

Wally nodded.

"Are you the one?"

"Am I the what, Flora?"

"The gentleman."

Wally wondered if he had overplayed his part. "It's a very complicated situation," he said. "The utmost secrecy, you understand. On no account must the lady in question know anything."

"No, sir," said Flora eagerly. "What mustn't she know?"

Wally spread out his hands. "I really can't tell you very much. Only that I'm very much in love. And very jealous." He paused.

"Husband, sir?"

Wally sighed.

"Let's just say another man. I need help," he went on. "Otherwise I'm . . . Letters, Flora. Anything you can find. I've got to know the truth."

Wally felt he had exhausted his display of melodrama. The girl was his.

"Now, should you wish recompense . . ."

"Certainly not, sir."

"To tell you the truth, I took one look at you and knew you weren't that kind of girl. Can you tell me anything?"

"Mrs. Neele arrived with nothing but a hand valise. But she keeps it locked."

Wally raised an eyebrow. "Done a little investigation already?"

"I wouldn't say that."

"Best to keep all this between you and me. Might jeopardize your job if anyone found you snooping."

The girl looked upset.

"Don't you worry. My life's in your hands and I won't give you away."

"Well, sir, Mrs. Neele's always at her desk. But no letters have arrived for her as I know. Course she's done a fair bit of shopping. Dresses. Antique tables. Lamps. A good number of books. One of them's called *The Phantom Thumb. And,* sir, she arrived with a large bottle marked 'Poison.' Maybe she did her husband in?"

"Good gracious no. Any idea what kind of poison, Flora?"

"No, sir, but I'll have a look."

Wally shook his head. "I expect it's medicine of some sort. Now not a word to anyone. Make a thorough search if you can, but be careful. If she thought I was prying she'd never speak to me again."

Half an hour later Wally went down to the porter's desk. "Been right through every company, Mr. Baring. None of them is holding any trunks for Mrs. Neele. Can't have been Leeds."

Wally shook his head. "Must have been Manchester," he said. "Thanks all the same."

He walked along the corridor to the Winter Garden. One or two tables were occupied in the dim green light. He thought the elderly guests looked particularly dismal as they waited for the dinner hour. Teresa Neele was not among them. But he found Evelyn Crawley with Oscar Jones and his uncle, and he was immediately asked to join them.

"Mrs. Neele back from Leeds?" he asked.

"I don't believe so," Evelyn said.

"I hope she doesn't stay overnight," Oscar interjected. "We're off to Mother Shipton's Well tomorrow morning and she promised she'd come."

Wally offered Oscar a cigarette. "More ghastly water?"

"Oh, no, Mr. Baring. Magic." Oscar rolled his eyes. "Mother Shipton was a sorceress. Lived in the fifteenth century and made very accurate prophecies. Described motor cars, steam engines. Local people used to consult her about their future. Nowadays people go there to make a wish. Miss Crawley's coming. Mrs. Neele seemed very keen. Why don't you join us, Mr. Baring?"

"I'd be delighted to," Wally said.

"Mother Shipton's Well," grumbled Uncle Jones. "That's gungel!"

"I know it's silly, Mr. Jones," Evelyn said, patting the old man on the arm. "But it'll be fun. We'll all come back and tell you about it and you can have a good laugh."

"A good laugh's not his forte," said Oscar under his breath.

"Speak up, lad," said Uncle Jones.

"Don't see why I should," Oscar replied and there followed a petulant quarrel between the two.

Wally leaned slightly toward Evelyn. "Mrs. Neele never went to Leeds," he said.

"What do you mean?"

"I thought I'd help out. Got the porter to check every shipping agency from South Africa. None of them has ever heard of her." He saw how he was upsetting Evelyn and lowered his voice. "We both know she's in trouble. Now why would she lie?"

"You could be mistaken."

Wally shook his head. "She may be in shock. You know her husband died recently." Wally trod carefully. "She's a lovely lady, and she trusts you."

"Yes, I know."

"Well, in my view, Miss Crawley, she needs a lot more help than she's getting. You're an intelli-

gent woman. I know it's presumptuous of me to
say this, but you should try to find out more about
her."

"You seem very keen on good works," Evelyn
said.

"Oh, no. I just find Mrs. Neele very attractive." He looked his pretty companion in the eye.
"I'm attracted to the wounded, especially when
they look like Teresa Neele. Unfortunately, she's
not too keen on me." He smiled brightly. "Trouble with you, Miss Crawley, you're terrific to look
at. Only you're one of the most balanced people
I've ever come across."

"That's a very confident judgment," she answered, "considering you hardly know me."

Both of them were now aware that Oscar Jones
was listening to their conversation.

Wally stood up. "Time to dine. You can usually tell because the guests rise like Lazarus and
actually run."

"Not all of them," said Oscar, raising his eyes to
heaven as he maneuvered his uncle's wheelchair
in the direction of the door.

Wally and Evelyn followed him through the
jungle of potted palms. Wally whispered, "Boy's
mad about you."

Ⓐ

Agatha had not taken off her coat, although several hours had passed since she had returned from
the Royal Baths. She lay on her bed, profoundly
exhausted. Even to turn on her side or reach for
a glass of water was an untolerable effort. Sleep
was denied her by a nagging, familiar anxiety. For

the first time since she had left Styles, she wanted to renege on her decision, to take the plan to pieces and seek some easier way.

Charlotte Fisher had called Archie her "adversary." That truth had not impinged on Agatha. Stronger than her physical need of him, stronger than her loss of a one-time good companion, stronger even than her fear of how a divorce might harm her daughter was her terror of being separate. That she and Archie were joined for life was a fact, absolute and unalterable, like the ties that bound her to her parents.

Long ago she had written a letter to Archie that began: "I know of no other experience which confers so much grace as loving and being loved by one person." When he wrote back, he told her that she thought too much about such things, that he preferred her jolly rather than pontifical.

There was no doubt about it, they had had a jolly time. Agatha restrained her show of feeling and concentrated on what she was exceedingly good at: being a playfellow.

Then Archie's business life, and his devotion to golf, began to occupy more and more of his time. The two companions played less and less. Agatha wrote, read, gardened, and took care of her child. She was not consciously aggrieved, and she began to practice self-sufficiency while still believing herself to be dependent. She was padded by self-deception, so that she missed the danger signals. When her husband told her he had fallen in love with another woman, that he wanted a divorce, she had lost her wits and her health.

Now, months later, like an amateur mechanic,

she was reassembling the parts—brain, body, heart.

Sometime after seven that evening, Flora opened the door of Room 182, switched on the light, and went to turn down the bed. Agatha sat up guiltily.

"I'm sorry, ma'am. Didn't know you were resting."

Flora wondered why Mrs. Neele hadn't taken off her coat and hat. In the bright overhead light, she saw that the woman's face was chalk white.

"Are you feeling poorly?"

"Bit of a headache, Flora."

"Would you like me to bring you some tea or some hot soup?"

"No, thank you. I'd like you to get a message to Miss Crawley. Leave it at the desk. Tell her I was delayed and I shan't be able to join her for dinner."

"Certainly, Mrs. Neele. Should you see a doctor?"

"That's not necessary," Agatha answered.

When Flora left the room, Agatha undressed and climbed into bed. Anxiety gave up its vigilant hold on her. She fell asleep and dreamt of a midday summer beach, of lying on the sand alongside Archie. She awoke smiling in the sensation of happiness. She lay awake till the cold early-morning room and her own familiar fear shut out the dream. She grabbed at sleep again, dreamt she lay beside her husband on a platform, reached to touch him and fell. Watched a corpse wheeled on a stretcher along an institutional corridor, past open doors leading to empty rooms. When ice-grey light awakened her, she tried urgently to remem-

ber if she had been the body on the stretcher or
just a spectator.

The dining room was even emptier than usual
at 8:00 A.M. A few backsliding guests, secret morning eaters reluctant to take the punishment of
sulphur water and brisk exercise were the only
occupants.

Miss Crawley sat with Oscar Jones and waited
for Teresa Neele. Evelyn had sent up a message
to her friend, asking her to be ready to leave by
nine.

Wally Stanton joined them. He ordered coffee,
toast and marmalade. He had brought an old
tweed coat and a cap. "What else do I need? Bin-
oculars? A map? Firearms?"

Evelyn smiled.

"Is Mrs. Neele coming too?"

"She said she would."

"She may not like the idea of my joining the
party."

"She has very good manners," Evelyn said. She
liked Wally more than she cared to admit, liked
his ease. He said he was in textiles, and she guessed
he was rich, but his background was no threat. He
was an American. She had no idea from where.
She hardly cared. There was no secret code of
behavior to be cracked with an American. For a
girl from the working class, it meant you could
lower your defenses. Evelyn minded that he liked
Teresa Neele more, but she was far too generous
to impede that preference.

Oscar had long ago finished his breakfast and

was studying a map. "Oscar's in charge of the expedition," Evelyn said.

The boy nodded. "First the moors!" he said. "Finest countryside in England. Then we double back to Mother Shipton's Well." Oscar took out a pencil and began to trace the route.

Wally poured himself more coffee. "Mrs. Neele must have got back rather late last night."

"I think so," Evelyn said. "She went straight to bed, so she did go to Leeds after all."

"Don't think so," Wally answered. "Perhaps it was Manchester." He looked at his watch. "Hadn't we better send the porter up to Mrs. Neele? Don't want to upset Mr. Jones's schedule."

"I'll go myself," Evelyn said and stood up. Wally followed her to the door of the dining room.

"She doesn't care for me, Miss Crawley. And . . ."

"You like her."

"Exactly. I want to ask you a favor. Could you manage to leave me alone with her?"

Evelyn paused, then gave a sharp little nod of acquiescence. She went up the stairs to the first floor and knocked on Agatha's door. Her friend was dressed and ready to set off. "Sorry I'm late."

"You look a little pale, Teresa." They walked along the corridor to the staircase.

"Hopeless love," Evelyn said.

"I beg your pardon?"

"Your brooch. You should give it to Mr. Baring. He's mad about you."

"Oh, I don't think so." Agatha changed the subject. "Gruesome day yesterday," she said.

"Was it Leeds or Manchester you went to?"

"Leeds," Agatha answered.

"Any luck?"

"No. They don't seem to know anything about me or my luggage."

"Well, that explains it. Poor you."

"Explains what?"

"How pale you look. Mr. Baring's coming with us. Is that all right?"

Agatha paused. "Not particularly. I find him a bit . . . pushy."

"I'm not joking. He really fancies you."

Agatha looked at her friend in surprise. "Are you sure? I thought he was just rather inquisitive. Americans often are. I certainly don't wish to be fancied."

"Perhaps you don't," Evelyn said, "but you look a treat."

Oscar and Wally were waiting in the hall. The four of them went out into the sunlight and climbed into a waiting taxi. Evelyn sat between Agatha and Wally inside the cab and Oscar took the seat next to the driver. He was cut off from his friends by a glass partition that refused to slide open more than an inch.

"Where's the game pie and the white-gloved servants and whatever else one expects on the moors?" Wally asked. "Can we trust Oscar?"

"If we'd gone to Mother what's-her-name's cave first," Agatha said, "we could have made our wish for game pie and all."

"With me in the white gloves," Evelyn said.

Agatha laughed. "You'd make a very pretty serving maid."

"And I have the right credentials."

"Where'd you get them?" Wally asked.

"From my parents," she said. "They were in the white-gloves business. But Teresa's used to game pie and that."

"In South Africa?" he asked.

"I used to live in England," Agatha said.

"Really? So you're not really South African?"

"No," she answered easily. There was something about the bright morning and the promise of a journey that had flapjacked her from despair to high spirits.

"Are you a huntin' and shootin' sort, Mrs. Neele?" Wally asked.

"Not really. I just like game pie and picnics. Preferably in comfort. And Oscar's forgotten our fur rugs."

The three of them waved at Oscar from the other side of the partition. The boy worked to open it and failed. He mouthed information through the glass and pointed out landmarks.

"Are you a grand American?" Agatha asked.

"Very," Wally said. "My sort of picnic would be a trout caught with a hickory stick and baked over a wood fire. Can of beer kept cold in the stream. Straw hat, barefoot. You know, that kind of American."

"The ones that become president," she said, playing along.

"Yes."

"Of textile firms?"

"Well, not quite president," he said, looking her in the eye.

"What's the name of your firm?" Evelyn asked.

"Baring, Baring and Baring."

"Really?"

"Of course not. I'm trying to impress you, Miss Crawley."

"Import business?"

"Yep," he said. "Buy it here and sell it wholesale."

They were now some way out of Harrogate and driving west through rolling, copper-colored moors.

"It's exceedingly beautiful," Agatha said. The other two agreed and smiled at Oscar, who was pointing out a large lake as if they might have missed it.

"He behaves as if he owns all this," Evelyn said.

"Whereas it probably belongs to Baring Brothers," Agatha added.

Wally knew he had to deflect Agatha's curiosity.

"If you were as rich as I pretend to be," he said, "how would you spend your money?"

"I'd buy houses everywhere," Agatha said. "They'd be deliciously comfortable, with well-planned gardens. Everything would be kept up perfectly and I'd move from one to another so there'd be no need for dustcovers."

"Just like J. P. Morgan," Wally said. "He had a place in London. Insisted that every evening the servants turn down the bed, adjust the nightlight and place a glass of warm milk on the bedside table. Every night of the year, though, he was usually at one of his other twenty-odd houses."

Both women laughed. "I want to buy houses, grow prize dahlias and find my relatives," Agatha added. "Evelyn wants a ride on a camel. What do you do with your wealth?"

"If I were rich, I'd leave Baring Brothers, go to Paris, and sit in a café all day and write."

"Oh, yes," Evelyn said. "Short stories."

"Maybe a mystery novel. Do you like detective fiction?" He looked at Evelyn.

"Not particularly. Teresa does, don't you?"

"I do, rather," she said.

"Sherlock Holmes?"

"He's the master," she answered.

"Dorothy Sayers?"

"Yes. But I do read other kinds of books, you know. I can even manage T. S. Eliot." She smiled.

"I'm sort of fascinated by crime," Wally went on. "Suspect there's a severely repressed criminal drive somewhere in me. Could that be the case?"

The women looked skeptical.

"You don't think I'm dangerous? It's the short, gentle ones you should worry about."

"Oscar'd make a good murderer," Evelyn said.

"But he'd want to tell all, don't you think?" Wally said.

"Most murderers usually like to show off."

"But you wouldn't *believe* Oscar," Agatha said.

"What fascinates me," Wally continued, "is the need to be caught. Don't you agree? When people do . . . irregular things, they ask to be caught. Take the Leopold and Loeb case. Now those two boys committed a highly successful murder."

"What did they do?" Evelyn asked.

"They were teen-agers, both from wealthy families, and they kidnapped and killed a boy called Bobby Franks."

"They wanted to commit the perfect crime," Agatha said.

"That's right. Only one of them, Leopold, left a pair of glasses behind, his own glasses, and they were a special kind, prescription, that could be easily traced. So I guess he wanted to be found—and he was. I sort of feel sorry for them."

"Nonsense," Agatha said. "They deserve to die."

The force of her statement unbalanced the lightness of the mood, and the three fell momentarily silent.

Then Wally said, "Well, I'd like to write about a similar story. I'm not sure I'm original enough to think up my own plot."

"It could have just been stupidity on Leopold's part, or an accident," Agatha said. "There could even be a very straightforward explanation that you haven't thought of."

The car came to a halt at the crest of a hill and Oscar jumped out to explain to the others that they must admire the view. The four of them stood by the side of the road, buffeted by a strong, sweet-scented wind. Below them was a black gully and beyond that a great range of moorland that stretched to the horizon.

"Not a house in sight," Oscar shouted against the wind. "Just thousands of sheep, and we're a stone's throw from some of the biggest industrial towns in the country!"

"It's champion," Evelyn said enthusiastically.

Agatha caught Wally's eye and laughed. He noted that the sharp air had brought color to her pale skin. He had an uncanny feeling that she felt happy.

"Now, if you were a poet, Mr. Baring . . ."

"But I'm not."

"Did you say you'd published anything?" Agatha asked him.

"One or two short stories." They were walking briskly along the side of the road.

"In a book?"

"Oh, no, *The Stanford Owl*," he said, inventing the name of a magazine. "The college paper. Then a friend of mine in New York started one of his own. He printed some of my stuff. Think he thought my family would back him. It was years ago," he pursued the invention. "I drank a lot, wrote rather little, and used up my allowance. When things got very bad, I was hauled back into the fold with the other sheep."

Evelyn laughed. "I didn't know you were wool. We're wool, the firm I work for."

Wally cupped his hands, baaed loudly, and the field of sheep baaed loudly back. The others burst out laughing. "In the blood," Wally said. "I can make sheep mad. I can cause mass hysteria among sheep."

Oscar looked at his pocket watch. "Off we go," he said. When they got back to the taxi, the boy took out his map and indicated the road to Knaresborough. The old Yorkshire cabbie regarded him with composure. "I know the road, sir. It's my job to drive foreigners around these parts."

He reversed his car and headed east. Wally now sat between the two women. He felt he had won some sort of confidence from Agatha.

They had to get out of the taxi and walk down an avenue of beeches to reach Mother Shipton's

Well. Wally bought four tickets, and the party entered the dank cavern, which glistened with water. The place was empty. "You put your hand in the well," Oscar whispered, as if he were in church, "and then you wish. Don't tell a soul or you break the spell. You take the lady's hand," he continued, taking hold of Evelyn's, "and place it in the water."

"Better get my glove off," she said.

Very gently Wally took Agatha's bare hand. She resisted. In the dim light he saw she looked terrified.

"You wish," she said. "I don't go in for that kind of thing."

"Nor do I," he said.

"What's next?" He turned to Oscar as if he weren't aware of Agatha's distress.

"Now we go to the Dropping Well," said Oscar. They followed him outside another cave, where, suspended in the cascade by invisible copper wires, were baby's shoes, stuffed birds, dolls, feathers, gloves, each object coated by lime and petrified by the high calcium content of the water.

Wally stood by Agatha while Oscar attached one of Evelyn's gloves to the wire.

"Want to petrify anything, Mrs. Neele?"

She shook her head.

"It's so sad," she said, while Oscar laughed loudly and urged Evelyn to hang his tie in the water.

"I bet he has that good feeling all the time," Wally said quietly to Agatha. "He must be dumb."

She nodded. "Could we go?" she asked.

They walked out ahead of the other two and

back along the avenue of beech trees toward the taxicab.

"Thank you for getting me out."

"It was horrible," he said. "The morgue at Harrogate might have been more fun."

They walked on in silence.

"Perhaps you're better than you think," she said.

"I don't understand."

"Better as a writer, Mr. Baring." She began to gesticulate as if the matter truly concerned her. "I believe it's a question of practice. If you care enough."

Wally looked at her.

"Do you know that you use your hands a lot when you're not trying to cover up?"

She was instantly embarrassed.

"You're very personal."

"I'm American. We're not really acceptable. I apologize. I'm just very touched that you," he smiled at her, "bother to take an interest."

"Well, it's obviously important."

"Oh, yes," he said. "If you can do something well, really well. That's important."

"For a man, it's important," she said.

He looked at her again.

"That's the silliest damned thing I've heard you say."

Chapter 9

On the same Sunday morning that Agatha Christie visited a well in North Yorkshire, and refused to make a wish, a search began for her body in the area of Newlands Corner in the South of England.

By eight-thirty in the morning, hundreds· of volunteers had already arrived at the point of assembly high on the North Downs. They came in response to a police request for help. The fields were deep in mire, and a ground mist held well into the morning. By nine, Superintendent Kenward had set up his command post and sent out five hundred police of several counties to three points of assembly: Clandon Waterworks on the London-Egham Road at the foot of Newlands Corner, One Tree Hill on the Merrow Downs, and Cord Kitchen Lane on the Guildford-Reigate Road.

By midday three thousand cars had converged

on the area, along with thousands of cyclists. Eighty members of the Aldershot Motorcycling Club were out at their own expense. Throughout the day fleets of coaches brought amateur detectives to the site. Many cloth-capped workingmen and their families had come from London for a Sunday jaunt. There were farm boys in corduroys and leggings. There were local gentry, some of them mounted, some on foot. Women wearing plaid skirts, jackets, cloche hats, scarves and Wellington boots, and bearing stout staves, turned up to beat the undergrowth in search of the missing novelist. There were forty airedales, six bloodhounds, and many Alsatians trained in police work. There were university students just down from Oxford and Cambridge for the Christmas vacation. Mr. Gilling, the Sunningdale pharmacist, was out. So was the stationmaster. Jennifer Grummit, her pin head sitting on a pyramid of clothing, kept close to Kenward's elbow and took notes. From time to time she served him sandwiches and hot coffee from a Thermos. John Foster was there, wearing a borrowed oilcloth over his frayed tweed coat. His replacement on the *Sunningdale Echo* was busy interviewing one and all, as were huge numbers of the national press corps. John felt bitter about the fellow who had replaced him. To buck himself up, he too made notes—for Wally Stanton.

Sunningdale village turned out in force. Two notable exceptions were Charlotte Fisher, who stayed at Styles to look after Rosalind Christie, and the Colonel himself, who was far too angry to make an appearance. He failed to understand how Kenward had managed to mobilize the constabularies of four counties in the search. He knew for a fact that the Surrey force did not hold with Kenward's theory of foul play. One top man there had expressed the view that Mrs. Christie had undoubtedly spent the night warmly wrapped in her fur coat, left the car between four and seven in the morning, and walked to Gomshall and Shere station to catch the London train.

Archibald Christie also knew he could hardly complain about the massive search without drawing further suspicion on himself. But he was baffled. He knew the police held Charlotte Fisher's letter from his wife. He knew about the local rumors. But what real evidence was there to back up Kenward's spendthrift and publicity-seeking enterprise?

Only Foster knew that the Superintendent held the document which, whether genuine or not, was one of the incentives to the vast operation, the macabre holiday outing in search of a corpse.

Luland had opened his café on the crest of Newlands Corner, even though it was the Sabbath. He was doing a roaring business. Outside the café, Police Constable Reynolds was in charge of traffic. He was trying to deal with chaos. A fashionably dressed young woman with an equine face drove up to him in an open car. In the back seat of her Hispano Suiza were two bloodhounds.

"Who's in charge here?" she asked him.

"Superintendent Kenward, ma'am. Over there."

"Looks a poor show. No organization. You tell Kenward I need something belonging to Mrs.

Christie, a scarf or something, then I can put my dogs to work."

"Yes, ma'am," said Reynolds.

A mile down the road three golfing ladies had stopped for a smoke. One of them let out a deafening bellow.

"Nana! Heel!"

After a second or two, a black spaniel rushed up to her holding a mud-spattered handbag in its mouth. The woman took it and opened the bag.

"Nana, you *are* a clever girl." She took out a handkerchief and two receipts.

"Harrods," she said. "Must belong to Mrs. Christie."

Two amateur detectives who were watching rushed up to the group of women.

"Try and get your dog to lead us back to where the handbag was found," someone suggested. The little group plunged excitedly into the thicket, one or two of them sinking knee deep in mud and having to be hauled out, seeming to enjoy the exercise. Several police were called to the area and two farmers got to work with spades. They were unlucky.

Meanwhile, Kenward had enlisted a party of horsemen to carry instructions to the extreme flanks of the search party and bring back information.

The sun made a desultory appearance. Two Oxford men sat down on a fallen tree trunk to enjoy a packed lunch. "It's like Epsom Downs on Derby Day," one of them said.

"Lower orders mild as lambs."

"In search of a lady from the upper orders," the other one added. "They wouldn't have come out like this if she weren't famous."

"Of course not," the second boy said, opening the picnic basket and handing out a drumstick to his companion. "Damned silly place to be eating a chicken leg."

The two sat in silence for a while and watched the crowd surge past.

"At least they have bathtubs to put their coals in now," said the first young man. "Knowledge increasing, better social conditions, human power expanding. I'm very optimistic."

The other boy, who was coping with the contents of the picnic basket, shook his head. "There'll be a crash. What we need is a complete readjustment of the political system of Europe."

"I read that somewhere," said the first young man. "Oh, *I* know," he continued, "it was H. G. Wells."

"Usually is," said his friend glumly. "He's right, of course."

"Not in my view. I'm very optimistic about our political future."

The pessimist's attention was waylaid by a passing girl. "There's that girl again," he said pointing her out. "Pretty face but thick ankles."

They went on chewing their chicken.

A Tiger Moth flew low over the crowd and Kenward turned angrily to a mounted policeman. "Tell that fellow to work systematically, Jim. Tell him to stick to instructions. Pilot thinks he's performing for the bloody crowd."

Miss Grummit handed her boss a cup of tea

and gave one to John Foster. "That Mr. Stanton hasn't been in touch with me yet, John. Thought he wanted to meet me."

"Oh, he does, Grummit. You're on his list."

John turned to Kenward. "Any luck?"

"Not yet. But we'll find her. The body's somewhere in the area."

"Think there was a fight and he did her in?"

The Superintendent said, "They fired you, didn't they, Foster?"

John nodded. "Somebody in London brought influence," he explained.

"Thought as much," Kenward said. "Well, they won't bring influence on me."

"What if she's not here, sir? What if you're wasting your time?"

A reporter from London interrupted them. "How many people are out today, sir? What's your guess?"

"About fifteen thousand," Kenward said.

"Whole operation must be costing the public a pretty penny. Any idea how much?"

Kenward hated the press. He felt he was on to the truth and nobody was going to deflect him.

The reporter pursued him. "I'd say this was the biggest search of its kind ever undertaken in the history of this country."

"That's as may be," said the Superintendent and turned his back.

He continued giving instructions to his team of outriders. He had them organize small groups to move shoulder to shoulder across the terrain. He worked through the afternoon and into the early evening. When the light began to fail,

flares were lit to guide searchers who had lost
their bearings. By 6:00 P.M. the plateau had begun to empty, and the cars and coaches formed
a long line on the London road. John Foster sat
with Jennifer Grummit, waiting for the operation to end. He told her stories of the British raj,
half remembered from his childhood in India,
some of them not his own.

"She jawabbed him," John said.

"Jawabbed?" she asked, filling his mug with
tea.

"She was unfaithful," John explained. "So this
sepoy chopped off her hands. She stood there outside her hut holding out her two bound up
stumps for everyone to see, not saying a word.
The flies settled on them in the heat, and she
didn't move a bleedin' inch."

"Then what?"

"Her husband got off scot-free. A week later
some fellow stole a regimental chicken. He was
ordered to be whipped. Funny, really."

They sat in silence for a while, watching ghost-
ly figures in the night mist.

"No sign of the lady," Miss Grummit said.

"Nor the Colonel."

"He's getting off scot-free like your sepoy. That's
what the Superintendent thinks."

"I think Kenward's barking up the wrong tree,"
John said.

"He's not one to make mistakes," said his secretary defensively.

While the search was breaking up at Newlands

Corner and the last of the amateur sleuths were finding their way by the light of flares to the main road, Agatha Christie was busy in her hotel room removing the electric socket from the wainscot. By her side was *Essentials of Medical Electricity* by E. P. Cumberhatch. She picked up the rheostat she had bought and examined its three terminals. They were marked *a, b* and *c* in her manual. She attached the wires to each brass nut and screwed them into the threaded shaft to make the wiring secure. Then, with the aid of some spare lead and her screwdriver, she connected the wiring of the rheostat to the wall plug and to a lamp. She switched on the lamp and turned the rheostat from high to low. Then she switched off the lamp. She disconnected the wire to terminal *b* so that the current from the mains bipassed it and flowed to terminal *c*. When she switched on the lamp, there was a flash of flame from the wainscot and all the lights in that section of the hotel went out.

While maids fetched candles to light the corridors, and an electrician was called to find the source of the trouble, Agatha sat quietly in the dark. She thought about Evelyn and John Baring, and about the wide Yorkshire moors, and how the day had opened a few cracks of light in her black despair. But the more she thought about the fine day she had spent, the more she wanted her own world back, the restitution of her married life as once it had been.

When the light came on again she picked up her notebook and wrote:

1. Nancy now understands how control panel works
2. Rheostat experiment: success

She heard a knock on her door and hastily hid her rheostat. Flora came in with an electrician. "Excuse me, ma'am, but I wondered whether you were the cause of the lights going out? I told them you'd been buying lamps and wiring."

Agatha grasped the lamp and stood up. "Yes," she said. "I think I've done something stupid." She looked at the electrician. "Perhaps you could help me put it right? I'm frightfully sorry."

While the young man worked on the wall socket, Flora turned down Agatha's bed. She began to tidy the room, hoping to spot something of interest.

"That'll be all," Agatha said. "You may leave the electrician here."

The girl looked crestfallen. Agatha smiled. "I haven't bought anything new, Flora."

The girl said good night and went off to find Wally Stanton. She knocked at his door and he answered it in his dressing gown.

"It's her lamp," Flora said.

"It's her lamp what?"

"That's blown the fuse. She was wiring her lamp up to the mains. Must have done the wrong thing."

"Have you seen a rheostat in her room?"

"What's that, sir?"

"A sort of clock. A piece of electrical equipment."

Flora shook her head. "No, sir. Nothing like

that, and I've had a good look. Unless she's locked it away." Flora stopped, disappointed with her own story. "Funny, really, to go around buying old lamps when you've just run away from your husband."

Wally laughed. "Well you're a very good spy, Flora. No letters or anything else of interest?"

"Nothing, sir. Nothing except some songs. One's called 'Angels Guard Thee.' Oh, yes, and some new books. They look medical to me. To do with her treatment, I think. That bottle, sir, marked 'poison'? You were right. It's some kind of medicine and most of it's gone."

Wally thanked the girl and sent her away. Then he dressed for dinner. He felt despondent, at the end of the road with his story, that the plot, such as it was, had been unraveled, and that it was time to deliver. He went down to the lobby and dialed the *Globe-Enquirer*. He asked for the news editor.

"Where the hell are you, Wally?" Briggs asked.

"I've found Mrs. Christie."

"So I gather."

"I'll tell you where I am when you promise to print the story."

"I want it, Wally. I think Dintworth wants it too. It's just too big for his scruples. You sure you've found her?"

"I'm sure."

"Then let me send a photographer."

"Not till you get Dintworth's okay in writing. And don't bother to trace my call because you'll be disappointed."

"I hope you're not in Surrey, Wally."

"No, I'm not in Surrey."

"Because fifteen thousand people went out today looking for Mrs. Christie's body."

"You're kidding. On whose instructions?"

"Police."

"Kenward?"

"Yes."

"He's nuts."

"You're sure you've got her?"

"I'm really sure. I'll call you tomorrow and if all goes well you can send a photographer up on the afternoon train."

"Up where, Wally?"

"Up here."

"The husband's put out a five-hundred-pound reward for her."

"Good old Archie."

"And the *Daily News* has offered one hundred pounds to whoever finds her."

Wally thought for a moment. "We haven't got much time," he said. "I'll speak to you tomorrow."

He put down the receiver. He sat in the booth for a minute or two and felt sick with himself. Sick that he wanted the story so much, and sick that it wasn't a "better" story, by which he meant more lurid. And sick because he intended to wound a woman he liked.

He walked out of the booth, climbed the staircase to the first floor, and looked for Room 182. He knocked on the door and Agatha opened it. She had changed into a white dinner dress and was doubling a long row of pearls around her neck.

"What on earth's the matter?" she asked.

"I want to talk to you."

"Well it's hardly the place."

"It's the only place, Mrs. Neele. I'm not going to try to ravish you, I want to talk to you."

Agatha's expression was one of surprise and innocence. The thought that he might have seduction on his mind had evidently not occurred to her. He was touched that such an intelligent woman should be so naïve. If he had told her she was beautiful, she would probably have reacted in the same surprised way.

"Do come in," she said. She stood awkwardly inside the room. "I simply can't imagine why we can't talk downstairs. First you follow me in the street, now you follow me into my room. Why are you so curious?"

Wally saw that he had made her nervous, suspicious that he had guessed her identity. She hadn't enough pride left to believe there could be any other reason for his interest in her.

"I'm sorry I followed you. You wanted to be alone."

"I need time on my own, Mr. Baring. I enjoyed our outing today, but I need time to myself."

"Because of your husband?"

She nodded.

"You loved him very much?"

"I loved him and I miss my family, so I'm anxious to find my . . ."

"Your relatives," he said, as if the matter were perfectly comprehensible.

Agatha felt reassured. She sat on the end of

the bed and Wally walked about so that he could observe the contents of the room.

He offered her a cigarette and she refused it. "I really enjoy being with you," he said. "One of the reasons you make me feel good is that you're the first person I've met who's unhappier than I am."

"You can't change your fate," she said in a matter-of-fact way. "Unless, of course, you have enormous courage. That's why you should write, Mr. Baring. You can invent it all."

"I'm not sure I have the imagination to be good enough," he said. "I can only observe."

"Perhaps you're not prepared to take the risk?"

"You're using your hands again," he told her. "Although I can't believe you actually care. Perhaps other people's problems are a diversion from your own?"

She smiled slightly. He saw there was no buoyancy left in her.

"I've always thought it strange," he said very gently. "No matter how many times we look in the mirror, it's impossible for us to see ourselves, those flashes that only others see. You reading me. I thought I was the champion."

"Or you reading me, Mr. Baring. Why on earth are you in my room?"

Wally took the plunge. "Because I suddenly wanted to ask you a lot of very personal questions." He rushed on before she could interrupt him. "When did your husband die?"

"Last summer," she said.

"Was he the only man you ever loved?"

"Yes."

"Well, now he's dead, Mrs. Neele. So you have to start again."

"Why ever should I do that?"

"Because you deserve to, so you should hurry up," he said. "Why bother with your relatives? Is that going to help? Is it one particular relative you're looking for?"

"Yes."

"Don't waste your time looking for someone out of the past."

She got up and opened the door.

"Now will you go?"

Agatha left the Hydro early the following morning and walked down the hill to keep an appointment with the resident doctor at the Royal Baths. Most patients at some point during their treatment were checked by the elderly physician. Agatha explained that, despite Mrs. Braithwaite's excellent attention, she was still suffering considerable pain in her lower spine and abdomen.

"If Mrs. Braithwaite hasn't found the solution, then I suspect you may be suffering from some internal trouble." He looked down at her notes. "No illnesses on the record, I see."

"That's what's so strange," Agatha said.

"Well, we'll examine you and go from there."

He took her pulse and blood pressure, and prodded her stomach. "Can't find anything the matter," he said.

"I certainly don't feel any pain now. Perhaps I'm just run down. Could you possibly recommend a tonic?"

He readily agreed and wrote out a prescription. He looked up and smiled at her. "Jolly nice to see a pretty young woman for a change. Most of my patients are as old as the hills. Get awfully crotchety, y'know, when you're old. You stay young and pretty, my dear."

Agatha left the doctor and walked into the main vestibule. She sat down at an empty table and examined the doctor's prescription. She took a slip of paper from her handbag and, imitating the doctor's handwriting, transcribed its contents onto the prescription. She noted that the color of the ink from her pen was bluer than that of the doctor's. She decided to take the risk.

Fifteen minutes later she walked into a chemist's shop and presented her prescription. She waited in fear till the man returned and handed her two bottles. He took out the poison book and told her to sign.

She asked for some soap and toothpaste so that the pharmacist should not see how her hand shook while she signed the book. Then she paid, picked up her purchases, and left.

Wally Stanton's morning was also busy. As he left his bedroom he was waylaid by Flora.

"Anything you want me to do today, Mr. Baring?"

"Don't think I'm doing too badly." He winked at her. "But keep me posted." He lifted his hat to dismiss Flora, but the girl ran after him.

"You know what I think, Mr. Baring? I think your Mrs. Neele is that missing novelist, Mrs. Christie. Looks exactly like her."

Wally stopped and turned around. "Not true,

Flora. You're allowing your imagination to get out of control."

The girl looked disappointed. "I just thought perhaps she'd run off and left her husband for you."

Wally shook his head. "I'm afraid not. She's not Mrs. Christie." He turned and walked off.

He knew time was running out. He gave himself twenty-four hours to engineer a meeting between Nancy Neele and Agatha Christie. He checked his watch halfway between the Hydro and the Pump Room, and broke into a run. It occurred to him that he was quite possibly the only man in Harrogate still capable of running.

Nancy Neele and her aunt were not to be found. He waited in the Pump Room until it emptied of the morning patients, then he walked to the Royal Baths. He told the booking clerk he had a message for Miss Nancy Neele and was informed that she was not expected till her nine o'clock appointment the following morning.

Wally took a cab to the Valencia Hotel and wrote out a message to Miss Neele. He tipped a page to take it to her room and said he would wait to see if the lady were in.

Shortly after, Nancy Neele walked down the stairway into the dingy brown hall. She wore her clothes in a manner that suggested she had taken no care in their choice. Her eyelids were swollen and her face was pale.

Wally jumped up to greet her. "Do forgive me arriving like this, Miss Neele, without warning."

She was holding his note.

"Not at all, Mr. Baring . . . How's your leg?"

"Much better."

She looked down at the note. "I really don't believe we're related."

"You're probably right," he said. "But Mrs. Neele is quite convinced you're her cousin. She's *seen* you, I gather, and she really wants to meet you. Thinks you may recognize her. If you'd care to be my guest at dinner— Well, first it would be a great pleasure, and second we could settle this problem for Mrs. Neele. You'd like her."

"I'm sorry," Nancy said. "I'm quite sure we're not related. As I told you, our family never had any cousins in South Africa. The lady must be—"

"I know," Wally interrupted. "But you'd be doing her a kindness. Her husband died recently, and I think she's feeling very bereft. Unlike you, Miss Neele, she doesn't have a future."

The girl looked miserable.

"Is anything wrong?" he asked.

"I'm a bit upset," she said.

Wally had the feeling she wanted comfort, wanted to talk to somebody more consoling than her frumpy relative.

"Sit down here," he said, indicating a chair.

The girl was reassured by his concern.

"What's the matter, Miss Neele? Trouble with your fiancé?"

"A little bit."

"Well, I'm sorry to hear it. You haven't changed your mind?"

She shook her head.

"Nobody'd want to lose a girl like you."

"Oh no," she said. "I expect it will be all right."

It was quite clear that Miss Neele thought the contrary.

"You're sure you won't dine with me tonight?"

"No, thank you. I don't think I'm very good company, Mr. Baring, and of course I'd have to bring my great-aunt and she's . . . she's a . . ."

"A bore?"

"Yes," the girl said.

"If you won't let me take you out to dinner," Wally said, "perhaps we can have coffee sometime when you're feeling better?"

"That would be very nice."

"Tell you what. Let's have coffee together tomorrow. Are you going to the baths?"

"Yes, but early. Nine A.M."

"In that case let's meet around ten A.M. In the entrance hall."

"I'll see you tomorrow, then," she said and stood up. "You've been very kind to me."

They shook hands and Wally walked out into the street. He bought a camera and some film, then returned to the Hydro. He went to the telephone booth and put a call through to Lord Dintworth. He knew he could not mention Nancy Neele—the press lord might inform Christie.

"Harry," he said. "Do you want the story?"

"You're sure it's Mrs. Christie?"

"Absolutely sure. Same lady you sent me to lunch with a couple of weeks back. I've bought a camera. I'm going to photograph her tomorrow morning and then get back to London as fast as I can."

"Why not photograph her today?"

Wally smiled to himself. "You've changed your mind, haven't you?"

"I'll print your story," Dintworth said.

"I thought you would. Duty to the public, I'd say, a story on this scale. But I haven't just found her, Harry. I have a story which concerns the mistress. Will you publish that?"

"Yes. If it's accurate, and decent."

"Of course it's accurate and decent—it's for the *Globe-Enquirer!*"

"Why can't we have the story now, Wally?"

"Because tomorrow it will be twice as good. If I fail tomorrow morning, then I'll telephone through what I already know. There isn't much time, but I think it's worth holding off."

"Well, good luck, old chap. No expense spared."

Wally put the telephone down and went upstairs to change for dinner. Under his door he found a note from Flora. Enclosed was a small drawing she claimed to have found in Mrs. Christie's wastebasket. It was a rough sketch of the inside of a rheostat.

Wally presumed that the drawing had something to do with the lamp incident of the night before, and dismissed it as of no significance.

When he had changed he went downstairs. He could have made the journey down to the lobby and right along the paneled corridor into the vast, green-dim Winter Garden blindfolded. He had asked Evelyn Crawley to meet him there, and was looking forward to sharing the contents of her brandy flask. He watched her as she made her way to his table, admired the swing of her short dress against her pretty legs, and wondered why he felt no urge to seduce her. Impotence of the heart *and* the groin, he said to himself by way of explanation. Then he got up to welcome Evelyn. "Awfully nice of you to join me," he said, looking around. "Usual gay crowd."

"You know," Evelyn said, indicating the band, "our Charleston hasn't had much effect on them. They've gone back to 'Maid of the Mountains.' "

When the elderly waiter saw Evelyn, he came over with two glasses of water and two empty glasses, which he placed on the table.

"Thank you very much," she said solemnly.

"What do you want me to do, gargle?" Wally asked.

"No, Mr. Baring. Brandy. I've got the old boy trained."

She filled the glasses from her flask.

"Look," Wally said. "I've spoken to that cousin of Mrs. Neele's. She's agreed to meet me tomorrow morning at the Baths around ten. I'd like it to be a surprise for Mrs. Neele. Could you get her there?"

Evelyn considered the plan. "Seems a good idea."

"But I think we should keep it secret. Mrs. Neele obviously wants to meet the girl, but something's holding her back. Perhaps it's shyness, as you said."

Evelyn nodded. "Miss Neele obviously doesn't think she's related."

"No, but she does come from Rickmansworth. It's all very odd, but a confrontation might resolve something for Mrs. Neele. It might be therapeutic."

"Yes, I agree. I have a treatment at ten, but I'll see what I can do. We might have to make it later in the morning, but I'll let you know."

Agatha spent the early part of the evening checking the details of her plan. Then she changed her clothes. She sat waiting for the dinner hour and idly thumbed once more through a pile of newspapers. She tore out a photograph of Archie at the wheel of his open car, with Rosalind and Charlotte Fisher in the back seat. She looked at it lovingly and then locked it into her case. Agatha thought of Archie with pity. Her only desire was to have him back, and instead she had exposed his life to a barrage of publicity. She searched elsewhere to make sure she had missed no quote from him. The newspapers were her last and only line of communication. She smiled grimly at his offer of a £500 reward for her recovery. Several papers carried photographs of him. She checked her watch.

She opened the Sunday edition of the *Globe-Enquirer* once more and read Wally Stanton's column, read it with half her attention. Her eye was caught by the small caricature of his face that accompanied the article. She looked at it for a minute or two, baffled by its familiarity. Then she guessed who John Baring was.

Agatha folded the newspaper neatly, put it on top of the others, took her bag and shawl, and walked down to the dining room. She took the empty seat at the table with Oscar Jones, his uncle, Wally Stanton, and Evelyn Crawley, and apologized for being late, since the group now shared a table as a matter of course.

"Took a bet you wouldn't be late, Mrs. Neele," said Uncle Jones, having consulted his watch.

"Gambling's a dangerous occupation," she said. "Was the soup any good?"

"Dreadful," said Uncle Jones.

"I had a friend," Wally interrupted, "who believed that gambling was the only way of failing honorably. It's true, I think. People who want to fail, gamble."

"You don't seem like a gambling sort of person," Agatha said affably.

"Oh *I'm* not. Too scared, Mrs. Neele. Just don't have that kind of panache."

"You have great panache," Evelyn said brightly.

He smiled. "Just flash in the panache," he said.

The waiter served the roast chicken.

"Also Mr. Baring writes," Agatha said. "But he doesn't often have the nerve to put it all on paper. A great pity." She looked at him in desperation.

Wally felt a little uncomfortable. He covered up by offering help to Uncle Jones, who was fighting a piece of chicken gristle with his knife and fork.

Later that evening, when the group moved to the Winter Garden for coffee, Agatha withdrew somewhat from the conversation, although not so much that her silence seemed awkward.

Oscar had proposed a moral problem. "If the National Gallery were on fire, and you only have time to save one painting and there is a cat squealing, a perfectly ordinary rather ugly cat scared out of its fur, what would each of you do?"

Agatha answered at once. "Quite simple. Evelyn would save the cat, Mr. Baring would have the imagination to save the painting. So would you, I suspect. I wouldn't go in at all."

Wally asked, "Who'd save the mice?"

"The mice," she said, "always save themselves."

The group sipped coffee and conversation petered out.

"Why don't you sing?" Evelyn said.

Agatha looked at her friend and then walked across the room to the orchestra. She smiled at the pianist and the leader. She asked if she might choose a song. The band waited while she looked through a pile of sheet music, selected what she wanted, and gave it to the pianist. She stood beside him and sang the words in a high and delicate soprano voice.

"I once lov'd a boy, a bonnie bonnie boy
I loved him, I'll vow and protest;
I lov'd him so well, and so very very well,
That I built him a birth on my breast."

The room became silent as she sang the Scots ballad.

"She looked up high, and she looked down low
The sun did shine wonderful warm;
Whom should she spy there but her bonnie,
    bonnie boy,
So close in another girl's arms,
So close in another girl's arms.
For I thought he'd been bound to love but
    one . . ."

Agatha stopped and turned to the pianist. "I can't go on," she said. "I've forgotten the words." He could see that there were tears pouring down her face and he said, "Don't you worry, my dear." She stepped down off the podium, and Evelyn Crawley came to meet her and led her out of the room.

Evelyn took her friend's arm and steered her along the corridor.

"You're in love. That's for sure."

"Yes, I am," Agatha said, and looked over her shoulder. "I made such a fool of myself in there."

"No, you didn't."

"You know something, Evelyn? All the clues to one's life come well in advance of the action. I missed all the clues."

"Where is your husband?" Evelyn asked gently.

Agatha lifted her hands as if the question were irrelevant. "I thought we were dancing the same steps," she said. "And I didn't realize . . . notice."

"Notice what?"

"That we weren't together. That we weren't getting on."

Evelyn led Agatha up the staircase. "Has that Miss Neele got something to do with it?" she asked.

"Yes, she has."

"Do you really want to talk to her?"

"Of course not."

"Then I should tell you that Mr. Baring's organized a surprise meeting tomorrow. Between you and Miss Neele."

They had reached the top of the staircase.

Agatha said, "Don't talk to him. Don't tell him anything about me."

"Of course not. You go to bed."

"Please, Evelyn. Don't go back and talk to him."

"I promise I won't. Now where's your key?"

The band had stopped playing. The saxophonist said to the banjo player, "It's her. I'm sure of it. That Mrs. Christie. She was singing as if we didn't exist. In her own world."

His friend nodded. "We'd best go to the police."

"It's that foggy out," the banjo player said.

"We'd best go anyway."

Wally Stanton smoked a cigarette or two and waited for Evelyn Crawley to return. An hour passed before he finally gave up and went to bed.

Chapter 10

She slept better than usual, did not wake in the early hours of the morning and run the course of a maze to which there was no exit, suffered no pain. Instead, she slept till 6:00 A.M., self-programmed to wake at that hour, and slid immediately out of bed. When Flora knocked and entered with early-morning tea, she found Agatha fully dressed and putting on her coat.

"You're up early, Mrs. Neele." The girl noted that the room looked emptier and that the desk was cleared of books.

"You're not leaving us, are you?"

"No, Flora. Waters as usual. Then I'm off to the Baths."

"Would you like a morning paper?"

"No, thank you," Agatha said. And the chambermaid had reluctantly to leave.

Immediately, Agatha bolted the door. She checked the room carefully, moved her incongru-

ous antiques into one corner, then went through
every drawer. From her small case she took a pile
of papers, examined them, then twisted and laid
them in the open grate. She lit a match and set
them on fire, crouching over the flames till the
papers were thoroughly charred. She checked the
remaining contents of her case. Then she put on
a pair of gloves, took the screwdriver from her
case, and wiped it clean of fingermarks. She put it
back, along with two technical books she intended
to dispose of elsewhere. Still wearing gloves, she
took the bottle marked poison, bought on the
previous day, and added it to her case. She did
up her coat, picked up the case, and left the room.

Agatha walked down the back stairs and left
the Hydro by the side exit. She walked half a
mile to the shopping area of the town and entered a public telephone box. She checked her
watch and noted it was just before 8:00 A.M.
She dialed a Harrogate number and put a coin
into the machine. When her call was answered,
she said, "Mrs. Braithwaite? Hello, it's Evelyn
Crawley." Agatha's voice perfectly imitated that
of her friend's.

"What can I do for you, dear?" Mrs. Braithwaite asked.

"I need your help. I just set out for a walk before my treatment and something awful's happened to my back. I'm in the public box outside
the hotel. I'm in agony."

"Well you'd better go back to your room. Can
you make it?"

"Could you possibly come to the hotel? I'm

not one to exaggerate, but I'm doubled up in agony."

"I don't know what to say, my dear. I've an appointment in an hour."

"I know, Mrs. Braithwaite, I telephoned the Baths first to find you. They gave me your home number. Said they could easily change your first appointment."

"Well, in that case, I'll be over as soon as I can," the therapist answered. "I'll try to find a cab but I won't be there for at least half an hour."

"I'm so grateful. Good-bye." Agatha put the receiver down and left the booth. She walked down the hill to the corner and posted a letter addressed to Evelyn Crawley. Then she continued in the direction of the Royal Baths.

Wally Stanton was worried. He knew time was running out, knew that Flora was incapable of keeping secrets, and must by now have told other people she thought Mrs. Neele was the missing novelist. Evelyn Crawley had not been in touch with him to confirm that she would deliver Teresa Neele to meet her cousin. He had sent a note to her room but had not as yet received an answer.

Although he had positioned himself on guard in the hall of the hotel at an hour when he would normally be still in bed, Wally had not seen Agatha. He tipped a page to deliver a message to her room and was told that there was no reply. Wally said that his message was of extreme importance and sent the boy to fetch Flora.

Nancy Neele stood in her bedroom examining

her figure in the long looking glass. She had not
lost much weight. Worry and loneliness had increased her appetite. Twice Archie had managed
to telephone her and on each occasion he had
seemed harassed and self-absorbed. The public
furor, the innuendo and invention that surrounded the disappearance of his wife, had taken
their toll. He knew no way to fight back. When
Nancy had begged him to let her return, he asked
her to stay in Harrogate because he feared the
press. He told her she must return neither to the
office nor to her family till Agatha was found. But
almost two weeks had passed and Archie Christie
was beginning to think that something serious
must have happened to his wife. Nancy gave him
what support she could while watching her future
crumble.

She took another look at herself in the mirror
and vowed to renounce all fattening food. Then
she dressed and walked to the Royal Baths for
her early-morning treatment.

Superintendent McDowell entered the Hydro
lobby with a colleague. Both were in plainclothes.
Though McDowell was in his forties, he was often
taken for a man of sixty. He looked old on principle. It suited the job and his authoritarian view
of life. He asked the receptionist to call the manager, who, once alerted, came rushing out of his
office.

"Good morning, sir. We think we've got her."

"Well, I hope you're right," said McDowell,
undoing the buttons of his overcoat. "It's only
the fourth time this week we've been called out

for the same lady. And we don't want to draw attention," he said, looking around the lobby. McDowell in plainclothes always drew attention. He and his colleague were unmistakably from the land of officialdom. The manager led them into his office. "It's not just my musicians, Superintendent. One of my chambermaids is convinced it's Mrs. Christie."

"First one of your musicians comes to my station at some ungodly hour, tells me Mrs. Christie got up and *sang*. In public. Ridiculous!"

"Leeming's a very reliable man. He thinks the lady's lost her memory. If she'd been aware of her identity, she might have been more self-conscious. But one of my chambermaids has got another story. She's willing to swear it's Mrs. Christie. Thinks she's perfectly normal and just hiding under another identity for private reasons. She's registered as Mrs. Teresa Neele of Cape Town."

"Is this woman in the hotel now?"

"She's not in her room," the manager said.

"Could I talk to the maid?"

Flora was summoned and came running.

"When did you conclude that Mrs. Neele was Mrs. Christie?" McDowell asked her.

"Well, sir, I've suspected it all along."

"Then why didn't you report it before?"

Flora thought quickly. "I wasn't sure. She arrived here with no luggage. That was odd to start with. After the second day, she behaved normally. I brought the newspapers to her most mornings, on her instructions. She read them very carefully. Once or twice I found her with swollen red eyes, as if she was upset."

The police officer sighed.

"*You* have a look at her," Flora said. "She fits the description, I promise you."

"Well, where is she?"

The girl looked worried. "She's not in her room. That's for sure. The odd thing is she was all dressed and ready to leave this morning when I brought her her cup of tea."

McDowell turned to his colleague. "Get Bill and Frank over here." He turned to Flora. "Not a word about my being here, miss. If you're right, and this lady suspects anything, she could slip out of our hands."

"Now," he said, "I'd like to search her room." The manager dismissed Flora and led the police officer through the lobby and up the stairs.

As Flora went along the corridor toward the door leading to the servants' quarters, Wally grabbed her. "Are those policemen?" he asked. She nodded. "Did you tell them Mrs. Neele was Mrs. Christie?"

"Mr. Leeming in the band told them first," she answered.

"Did you tell them about me?" he asked.

"No, I swear. As God's my witness."

Wally lost his temper. "You're not Mata Hari, you silly girl. Tell the truth!"

"I am telling the truth. I think your Mrs. Neele is Mrs. Christie, but I didn't tell them . . . that is, nothing about you being in love." Flora's declaration did not reassure him. As likely as not, she had ruined his story.

He turned suddenly and ran back to the lobby and up the stairs. The door of Agatha's bedroom was open and the hotel manager stood nervously on the threshold. Wally pushed past him. He rushed up to the police officer and demanded to know on whose authority the room was being searched. The Superintendent was crouching over the charred remains of some paper in the fireplace. He turned slowly around.

"I don't know who you are, sir, but on whose authority are *you* in here?"

"I'm a friend of Mrs. Neele's."

"How long have you known her?" McDowell asked, standing up.

"Years," Wally said. "Old family friend from South Africa."

"Well, we've been informed that your friend bears a close resemblance to the missing novelist, Mrs. Christie."

"That's crazy."

"It's my job to make sure." McDowell walked around the room, taking a good look. He picked up the papier mâché table. "Must have cost a fortune," he said.

Wally snatched the table from the policeman's hands. "You have no search warrant and therefore no right to examine the contents of this room. Mrs. Neele is not Mrs. Christie and not a criminal!"

The manager rushed between them as if to defend the huge policeman from the small reporter. "It's my hotel," he said, "and I have a right to enter any of the rooms."

Wally knelt down to look at the charred papers. They were too badly burned to be legible.

"Sorry, sir," said McDowell, taking hold of

Wally by the arm and directing him toward the door. "These are police matters."

Wally ran down to the lobby. He had to think fast before telephoning the *Globe-Enquirer*. Agatha's room had a deserted feeling. He had the strongest feeling she had left the town. He checked with the pageboy to find out if he had seen Mrs. Neele. The boy said that nobody seemed to have seen her.

She walked through the main hall and stopped at the clerk's desk of the Royal Baths. "Good morning." She smiled at the misanthropic clerk. "Mrs. Braithwaite still away? I'm Miss Neele."

The man checked the appointment. "Of course she's not away," he said irritably. "I expect she's waiting for you."

"Oh, good," Nancy said. She turned and walked toward the treatment room.

Evelyn stepped out of the lift into the hotel lobby. The pageboy saw her and said to Wally, "Perhaps Miss Crawley would know where Mrs. Neele is."

"Good idea," Wally said, and went over to the girl. "Why didn't you answer my note?"

"Was it so very urgent, Mr. Baring?"

"Is Mrs. Neele going to the baths, because that cousin of hers will be waiting."

"I don't think she wants to meet her cousin," Evelyn said. "So you'll have to cancel the arrangement."

"Mrs. Neele's in trouble," Wally said, taking hold of Evelyn's arm.

"I think you should leave Teresa alone. I don't think she—"

"Do you know where she is?" he interrupted. "Because it's extremely important that we find her immediately."

"No, I don't know where she is and please take your hand off my arm."

"Listen, there are two plainclothes policemen in the hotel. They're here now, waiting for your friend. They think she's Agatha Christie."

"Who?"

"The missing novelist. Several members of the staff went to the police. Think they recognized her, and they're right."

Evelyn thought very fast—of the shopping expedition and the discarded clothes, of Teresa Neele's curious advertisement and her confessions of the previous night. She felt chillingly sure that the information was correct.

"Are you a private detective?" she asked.

"Sort of."

"For her husband?"

"No, more or less independent. And I've got to talk to you."

"I'd rather talk to Teresa first."

"I've just been in her room. The police were searching it, and I rushed in and shouted that they had no right to do so. Her stuff is still there, along with a lot of burnt papers in the grate. Now where is she, because I've been hanging around since dawn on the lookout for her, and nobody's seen her."

"Independent detective. That sounds peculiar to me. And you could be wrong."

"Yes, but if I'm right and your friend's in trouble . . . She hasn't lost her memory, you know that. What's she doing here, following the mistress? What did she want from Nancy Neele? Don't just clam up, Evelyn," he said, calling her by her Christian name for the first time. "Was Agatha Christie trying to make some deal with the girl?"

Evelyn lost her temper. "She's not the kind of woman to make deals!"

"Keep your voice down, we're drawing attention," he told her. "If she hasn't made contact with the mistress," he went on, "then she's got to be crazy to come up here, using the same surname as Nancy Neele. She wants to *be* Nancy Neele, don't you see, so her smug, self-centered husband will love her." He paused for a second. "Is that right? Is that what it's all about? If there's any other explanation, then tell me."

Wally could see that Evelyn was considerably affected.

"I really can't talk to you. Teresa told me last night on no account to speak to you, so she must have guessed who you are."

"I'm a journalist," he said.

"Well, that's disgusting."

"No it's not. It's a job."

"She thought you liked her. *I* thought so."

"I do like her. But what if she has some kind of plan, what if she's up to something that even you don't know about?"

"I've got to find her," Evelyn said, and she turned to cross the lobby to the porter's desk.

Mrs. Braithwaite had just entered the hotel and was in hot dispute with the porter.

"Of course she's in her room," the therapist said.

"My page says there's no reply from her room."

"Then you must fetch the manager and open the door. Miss Crawley could be . . ."

At that moment Mrs. Braithwaite saw Evelyn and her expression changed from anger to surprise, and then to indignation.

"Well, my dear," she said, "you're clearly not flat on your back."

"Flat on my back?"

"You sounded as if it was an emergency! I wouldn't have come to the hotel unless—"

"But I never asked you to come."

"Now, Evelyn, you telephoned me at dawn, then you . . . Now what is this all about?"

"Mrs. Braithwaite, I did not telephone you at all!"

Wally interrupted. "May I help?"

"This young lady called me at eight A.M.," she told Wally, her voice full of baffled rage, "and told me she was in agony. Told me she'd called the Royal Baths and they'd canceled my first appointment, so I came over here and that poor Miss Neele will have arrived for *her* appointment and there may be nobody on duty to look after her. Now what a selfish thing to do, Evelyn! Quite unlike you."

Wally suddenly turned and ran toward the hotel exit. He ran all the way down the hill in the direction of the Royal Baths.

Nancy Neele knocked on the door of Mrs. Braithwaite's consulting room. There was no answer. She looked at her watch, then opened the door. She walked through the therapy area and into the changing room. A coat and dress were hanging on a wall hook, above a pair of shoes.

Nancy went back into the therapy room. As she entered, a woman's voice from behind the screen asked, "Is that you, Mrs. Braithwaite?"

"No, it's not," Nancy answered. "She doesn't seem to have arrived. Perhaps she's still not well."

"She's perfectly all right," the woman said. "She just left me in the chair."

"How strange," Nancy said. "I thought mine was the first appointment."

There was a short silence.

"Shall I try and find her?" Nancy asked.

"You'd better help me first," the woman said.

He ran till he could feel the pain across his chest, and all he could see in his mind's eye was his clue, a crumpled scrap of paper with an electric circuit crudely drawn in pencil, the clue that Flora had provided from Agatha's wastebasket. At the time it had made no impression on him.

He ran up the steps of the Royal Baths, through the revolving doors into the main hall, pushed past two people at the appointments desk, and grabbed the startled woman clerk.

"Is Mrs. Neele here? Mrs. Teresa Neele? It's very urgent."

A woman clerk was on duty. She looked down at her book. "We've only two people for the first appointment, sir. Miss Nancy Neele, and—"

"Where is she? Fast! Where *is* she?"

"Well, she's with Mrs. Braithwaite."

"Which room?" He was still gasping for breath.

"She's in number four. Would you like a message taken in?"

But before the clerk finished speaking, Wally turned and rushed toward the women's section of the Baths.

"Mrs. Braithwaite's set the rheostat and left me here. Would you mind turning on the current?"

All Nancy could see was an arm immersed in a cylinder of water.

"Are you sure I should?" she asked.

And the woman behind the screen said, "Quite sure. Hold the lever, then turn the switch to *On*. It's perfectly straightforward."

Nancy stood uneasily in front of the instrument panel.

"It won't hurt you," the woman's voice said.

Nancy flipped the switch to *On*.

Chapter 11

There was nobody about in the long vaulted corridor. And he ran. The clatter of his feet on the tiled floor cut into the noise of the blood pounding in his head. He turned a corner, clocking the numbers of the room as he went. Then a woman screamed. She went on screaming as Wally opened the door of Therapy Room 4 and ran through the consulting room to the treatment section.

The screen in front of the Schnee chair had been knocked forward and the full force of the current from the mains had jerked Agatha's arms and legs out of the cylinders of water and buckled her body backward. So strong had been the first shock that it had catapulted her limbs out of the cylinders, pulled the electrodes out of the water, and snapped the leads. She lay back, her eyeballs rolled up into their sockets, lay there straddled across the chair. She looked to Wally like a victim of the electric chair whom the executioner had forgotten to strap down.

"Switch it off!" he yelled at Nancy Neele. "How do I switch it off?" he shouted.

The girl pointed to the panel and continued to scream. Wally found the switch and turned it to *Off*, not knowing that the current had already been broken. He lifted Agatha out of the chair and onto the floor. He pulled her toweling robe together in a helpless, motherly way, as if to protect her from the obscene act she had allowed the other woman to witness.

He felt her heart, felt that its beat was faint and irregular. She was breathing very shallowly. He cradled her head, while Nancy Neele repeated hysterically, "It's Mrs. Christie. She told me to do it. Told me to switch it on. I didn't know she was behind the screen. I've killed her!"

Wally paid no attention. He leaned over Agatha and willed her to recover. He said, "Come back. Please come back." He kept his hand on her pulse.

He shouted to Nancy, "Get a doctor!" Then he said, "No, wait here." He could feel Agatha's pulse becoming more regular. He began to slap her face violently.

"Get some towels," he said over his shoulder to Nancy, who stood whimpering and shaking.

"I could have killed her."

"But you haven't," he said. "Get the towels, fast."

Nancy found some towels and Wally took them and rubbed Agatha's hands and legs dry. He took off her wet robe and wrapped the towels around her.

"Now go and get her clothes, and bring them here."

Agatha sighed and began to come to. Her eyes were starting to focus, although she looked at Wally without expression.

Nancy returned from the changing room with Agatha's clothes, shoes, and case.

"Miss Neele," Wally said, "you've got to get out of here fast. Not a word to anyone. You don't want a scandal, for God's sake." He looked over Agatha's clothes, took her coat, and forced her arms into it. He put on her shoes, and then stuffed the rest of her things into the hand valise.

"Now, get your coat," he ordered Nancy Neele, "and carry the case for me as far as the main entrance."

He searched the room and found a blanket. He wrapped Agatha in it, picked her up, and carried her through the Baths, with Nancy Neele walking behind him. None of the guests or personnel seemed concerned or even curious about the woman in a blanket being carried out of the building.

Wally lifted Agatha gently into a taxicab and took the valise from Nancy.

"Now get away from here as quickly as you can," he told her. He climbed in and told the cabbie to go to Valley Gardens. He held Agatha with one arm so that her head could rest on his shoulder. He noticed that the driver was watching him curiously in the rearview mirror.

Wally looked down and saw that Agatha's overcoat was open and that it was obvious to the man in the front seat that she was wearing no clothes underneath. Surreptitiously, Wally did up all the buttons with his free hand. He then dug into the case beside him and pulled out her cloche hat. As gently as he could, he tried to pull the wool cap onto Agatha's head but, with only one hand free, the operation was ludicrously unsuccessful.

Agatha watched him, still without expression.

"Anything wrong?" shouted the cabbie through the partition.

"My wife's ill," Wally said.

"Funny place to take her, Valley Gardens, if you don't mind me saying so."

"I've changed my mind," Wally shouted back. He leaned forward to check that the sign ahead advertised a hotel and then told the cabbie to draw up in front. The Green How, like the Valencia Hotel, was in a terraced row, and had the same unprepossessing look about it.

Wally paid the driver and carried Agatha out. "Can you stand up?"

"I think so," she said.

He put one arm around her waist and, as the driver held out the valise, pulled Agatha's hat further down over her face. Then he led her very slowly into the small vestibule of the hotel. "Room, please," he said to the man behind the desk. "The lady's sick."

The manager looked skeptical. "Double room?"

"Single will do," Wally said.

"On the cheap?" the man smiled unattractively.

"Just give us a room."

"I think a nice double one's what you want." He chose a key, took the valise from Wally's hand, and led the way upstairs. Wally carried Agatha up the single flight.

He put her on the double bed in the small room

and closed the skimpy unlined chintz curtains. By the time he had tipped the manager and closed the door, Agatha was already asleep. He saw that she was breathing regularly and covered her with part of the bedspread.

He left the room, locking the door behind him, and went to find something to drink. When he returned, Agatha was lying in the same position. She woke up as he came in and watched him carry two glasses and a bottle of brandy wrapped in a napkin across the room. He filled one and gave it to her.

"Come on. Drink it," he said. Wally lifted her up and made her take a sip. He pulled off her hat and threw it on the floor.

"I don't like alcohol."

"I know you don't. Drink some more."

"Thank you," she said in a low voice.

"I'd offer to take your coat but you're stark naked."

Agatha gave him a very slight smile, then almost immediately it faded.

"They should promote you, Mr. Stanton," she said without feeling. "Very clever."

"You're fairly sharp yourself," he told her. "Suicide's one thing, but to pin a murder on your husband's mistress . . ." He picked up the other glass and filled it. "Why did you do that?"

"I didn't do that—pin a murder on her," she said. "Ask Evelyn. I've written to her."

"You *used* Evelyn?"

Her face showed some fear for the first time. She said, "I trust Evelyn."

"And you abused that friendship," he goaded her.

"You did rather well yourself, with me."

"It's my job."

"Your job and my life."

"And Nancy's, possibly," he added.

"Oh, no," Agatha said, "never." She spoke slowly and with great effort. "I simply wanted to get her in my sights. I used to do that with the leopards when we went on safari. More sporting that way, but Archie disapproved."

She closed her eyes and he saw that her face looked clamped shut.

"Thing is, you were careless," he went after her again. "People in your state leave clues around, or cries for help. Now, if you'd strapped yourself into that chair you wouldn't be alive. Then there's that advertisement. Your books are much less careless than your life."

She opened her eyes. "My life's a disgrace."

Wally picked up Agatha's glass, and gave it to her. "Go on," he said lightly. "It's strychnine."

She made a movement to sit up. "No, it's not," she said, "it's arsenic."

He looked at her dumbly for a minute, then he realized what she meant. He grabbed her valise and pulled out her clothes. At the bottom was the bottle of poison. He looked at her with a sort of fearful respect.

"Not so careless," he said.

Agatha's eyes filled with tears. She turned away from him onto her side, covered her head with her arms, and began to sob.

"I'm sorry," he said. He moved up to her on

the bed, pulled her into his arms, stroked her hair, her cheek.

"Should I get you a doctor?"

"I'm all right."

"Just you cry," he told her.

"I've been crying . . . it feels for years."

Wally went on stroking her, cradling her head. After a while she turned her face to him.

"Was that a lie, too, about you wanting to write fiction?"

"No, but I'm not up to it. And you weren't up to suicide. I've been thinking about that bottle. I think if your plan had failed, and I hadn't interfered, well, I just don't think you'd have taken a slug of arsenic. You had to get somebody else to do it for you the first time." He went on stroking her. "You know something, you were scared to death to admit how strong you are, *who* you are? You're bright and funny and your own person. If you admitted that, you wouldn't want your husband any more."

"I do want him."

"Funny way to get him back, to try and kill yourself."

She cried some more and he made her drink the brandy.

"You don't want him back," he said. "Have you ever read *Anna Karenina?*"

She nodded.

"Well, I don't think Anna throws herself under a train for her lover. She's already made sure the affair won't work out. She can't bear the public disapproval because it hurts her sense of herself. If she'd been able to write, I bet *she* wouldn't have tried to kill herself . . . She might not have been happy but she sure wouldn't want to be dead." He stopped for a minute and then said, "I don't know what I'm talking about."

Agatha took the handkerchief he was holding and blew her nose. Then she covered her head again with her arm. She said, "I feel I'm in somebody else's nightmare, and when they wake up they'll be ashamed."

Wally was feeling bad about his hectoring. He went on stroking her. "When *you* wake up, you'll be fine," he said. "You'll rejoice."

Agatha lifted herself on her elbow. She said, in a resigned sort of way, "And you'll make a story out of it."

He slid his legs onto the floor and looked at his watch. "You're going to have to get dressed, Mrs. Christie, and go back to your hotel."

By lunchtime the lobby of the Hydro was buzzing with anticipation and activity. Superintendent McDowell and his plainclothes underlings lurked around the public rooms, looking acutely secretive. The staff and many of the guests at the hotel already knew that Mrs. Neele might be Mrs. Christie, and the lobby was unusually crowded.

Flora, who had been told to remain in the servants' quarters, had on several occasions crept out to see if the missing lady had returned.

Just after one, Agatha walked into the hotel. Her head ached severely and her vision was blurred. She moved as steadily as possible across the lobby, trying not to notice that all eyes were upon her. She asked the porter whether he had seen Evelyn Crawley.

"Probably at lunch, ma'am," he told her, looking nervously toward McDowell.

Agatha thanked him and went to the dining room. Immediately, the manager ran over to McDowell.

"That's the one."

McDowell nodded. "I think you're right."

"Are you going to arrest her?" the manager asked, uncertain as to whether Mrs. Christie would bring custom or disaster to the Hydro.

"Not till her husband's confirmed it," the Superintendent answered. "She's not a criminal, but we mustn't let her out of our sight." He looked at his watch.

"Local press are already here, sir," the manager went on. "What do I do about them?"

"We keep them away from Mrs. Christie. I'd better telephone the Colonel."

Seven or eight people sat at different tables in the dining room under the cold light that filtered through the glass ceiling. Agatha walked over to Evelyn, who was sitting alone.

"Where are the others?"

"I don't know," Evelyn said. "You look terribly ill. Hadn't you better lie down?"

"No, I need to talk to you, very urgently, before they . . ."

"I know who you are," Evelyn said. "And they're going to watch you till they've found your husband and brought him up here. Do you want something to eat?"

Agatha shook her head. She supported her head

with her hands to prevent herself from falling forward. "I tried to kill myself this morning, Evelyn. If I'd succeeded, you would have been implicated. That is, you might have had to testify, tell them I'd done it."

Evelyn began to shake. She covered her feelings by delving in her bag for her brandy flask and offering some to Agatha.

Agatha smiled wanly. "You're so practical. I try to kill myself, and everybody brings out the brandy. It's as if I'd fainted. Evelyn," she said, "I tried to *kill* myself. Do you want to hear me, or are you going to dismiss me with your stupid, heartless, blind practicality?"

Evelyn blinked. "Now listen carefully," Agatha went on, "and I'll tell you what I've done, or failed to do, because tomorrow you'll get a letter from me. And now I've got to try and cover it all up." She began to describe what had happened during the morning.

"So, you see," she concluded, "I'm in the most awful trouble. What shall I do? What will Stanton print? It will destroy Archie."

Evelyn had turned red in the face with shock and horror and anger. "What should you *do?*" she said. "I shouldn't think there's any more you can do!"

"I'm bitterly sorry," Agatha said.

"If you'd died, it would hardly have reflected well on your precious Archie."

"Then you would have produced my letter," Agatha said, fighting her exhaustion, "and everyone would know it was my fault."

Evelyn lost her temper. "I thought I was a

friend. Not some pawn in your plan. You worked this out in advance, that's what's so terrible. Can you imagine how I'd have felt if you had died?"

"They wouldn't have hurt you," Agatha said quietly.

"Come on." Evelyn got up. "Let's get out of here."

"I don't think I can move."

"Oh, yes you can. You're as strong as an ox," Evelyn went on angrily, steering her friend through the lobby, past the curious eyes of the crowd, and into the garden.

"There," she said, shoving Agatha onto a bench. "Now breathe deeply, and don't keel over or the police will be over here in a second."

Agatha rested her head on the back of the bench, feeling the keen afternoon air like a sharp pain with every breath.

"What will Stanton do?" she asked again.

"What does it matter? It couldn't be worse. Good God, you and your . . . your playacting, dramatizing your injuries. Hopeless love, that silly brooch." Evelyn got up and began to stride up and down in front of Agatha. "And all because of that ordinary girl and your pompous husband. If he's anything like he sounds in the newspaper reports, he must be unbearable."

Agatha let her head fall forward. "What will Archie do?" she asked.

"He'll come back. And he'll hate you for it." Evelyn sat down on the bench, her anger exhausted. "He's driven you mad," she said.

"I don't want to be alone, Evelyn. I can't manage it."

"You'll learn to manage it."

Agatha shook her head. "I can't face the loss . . . I fear that more than death."

They sat there, not speaking for a while, watching the two plainclothes policemen watching them. There was the sound of distant traffic and the odd mournful cry of a winter bird and the sour smell of chrysanthemums.

"I can smell your favorite flower," Agatha said.

Evelyn turned to look at her. "Lose him, and you'll never be frightened again. Come on." She helped her friend stand up. "Let's go to your room. You'll find somebody else to love," she said. "There's always somebody else."

The two policemen watched the women enter the hotel.

"Think we can go now?" The younger of the two blew on his fingers to get them warm. "I wouldn't say no to a cup of tea. Think it's her?"

"Not worth the trouble," the other man said. "Fancy wanting your wife back. Her husband offered five hundred quid for her!"

His colleague chuckled. "T'other one's a good-looking lass. Wouldn't say no to her."

The older man wasn't listening. "Five hundred quid." He shook his head. "Yer can't 'elp but wonder."

The London train pulled into the station at Harrogate at precisely 6:23 P.M. Archie Christie walked along the platform, past bright posters welcoming him to the spa town. He went through the barrier and out into the cold night.

He looked around as if he expected to be met, but no one approached him. He asked a porter how far the police station was.

"Up the hill, sir. Hundred yards on your left."

"I'll walk," Archie answered, though no alternative transport had been suggested.

He carried nothing but a briefcase because he had dashed to the station from his office to catch the early-afternoon train. He went into the police station and asked to see Superintendent McDowell.

"I'm Colonel Christie."

The young constable on duty sprang to attention. "Good evening, sir," he said. "We've been expecting you."

"Well, you weren't at the station," said the Colonel, testily. "Where's McDowell? I'd like to speak to him first, before I confront my . . . this woman."

"Quite understand, sir. The Superintendent's at the Hydro."

"Then I suggest you ask him to come over here to meet me."

The policeman picked up the telephone. Within ten minutes McDowell walked into the station and greeted Archie.

"We've got her, sir," he said.

"What do you mean, 'got her'? Have you locked her up?"

"Good Lord no, sir. But we thought we'd lost her this morning. Then in she walks at lunchtime. I've had her under my eye ever since. Of course, she doesn't know she's being watched."

"How did . . . how has she behaved?" Archie asked uncomfortably.

"According to the manager and several of the guests, this Mrs. Neele behaved perfectly normally. Seemed she made friends an' all. Proper lady, they say. You'd better come to the hotel."

"You realize if it is my wife, we must maintain the utmost secrecy. She could be suffering from . . . In any case, if it isn't my wife . . ."

"She looks like Mrs. Christie, sir. Though I spoke to my colleague Superintendent Kenward this afternoon, and he tells me I'm on a wild goose chase."

"Kenward's a fool," said Archie crisply.

"Well, shall we go then?" McDowell asked. He hoped the Colonel was correct, because he wanted to be the one to snare the missing lady.

The two men climbed into the waiting police car and were driven the short distance to the Hydro. The manager came out to meet them, led them into his office, and offered refreshments. His manner was solemn, even reverential, as if he had taken charge of a funeral. Archie asked a number of questions. He was told that Mrs. Neele had gone to her room and that a close watch was being kept on her. "Should she be brought down?" the Superintendent asked.

"I think not," Archie decided. "Might cause embarrassment if she isn't my wife. I'd rather wait in the lobby till she comes down for dinner. If she doesn't appear at all, well, then perhaps an approach should be made."

The three men went back into the lobby and stood awkwardly among the crowd of hotel guests already changed for dinner; many of them had gathered there to find out whether Mrs. Neele was the missing novelist. They stood about, admiring the lights on the Christmas tree, waiting in pleasurable anticipation, to witness a woman's private crisis.

Also in the crowd were several London reporters. Members of the hotel's staff had alerted them that morning in the hope of receiving a reward. The reporters had immediately journeyed north in pursuit of the hottest story of the day.

Shortly after 7:00 P.M., Agatha walked down the main staircase to the lobby. She was wearing a salmon pink Georgette dress with a rope of pearls doubled around her neck. She was carefully made up. Without looking around, she went over to the porter's desk and picked up an evening paper. She glanced at the photograph and front-page story on her own disappearance. Then she folded the newspaper and turned toward the corridor leading to the Red Drawing Room.

As she left the lobby, Archie caught up with her and called out, "Agatha."

She turned, smiled a little, and said, "Hello." Her greeting sounded casual.

"Where can we talk?"

"This way," she answered. He took her arm and they continued along the corridor.

"We must take the utmost care," he told her.

"Oh, we will," she told him. She said it with irony, although she felt nothing but astonished gratitude to have him back, the gratitude of a child who has carried out a threat and been taken seriously.

At the entrance to the corridor, McDowell and a colleague held back reporters.

"Later, gentlemen, please!" he shouted at the eager men. "We have to make sure it's Mrs. Christie."

Agatha and Archie turned into the drawing room, found it almost empty, and sat on a sofa by the wall.

"You've driven me mad," he said.

She listened calmly.

"I've been so worried. I know it was inconsiderate of me. I should never have gone off like that, left you in such a state. You had no idea what you were doing." He was not so much questioning her as stating the situation.

Agatha listened without interrupting him, allowed her husband to take charge.

"You do recognize me, don't you, Agatha?"

She nodded.

"You seem so calm," he went on. "You've obviously blocked a lot of things out of your mind."

While he spoke she was thinking how unfamiliar he looked, and how tired. For the first time since she had met him, she felt she could predict what he was going to do. He would take her back.

"Where did you get the money?"

"I don't remember. I have no idea how I got here."

"I should never have allowed you to drive while you were still so ill."

She went along with him, colluded, believed her own invention.

"You think I must have hit my head against the steering wheel of the car?"

"That's what happened," he said. "And those confounded policemen are still dragging the Silent Pool."

They both laughed nervously.

"Look," he said, "you've been suffering from amnesia. We'll have to tell them. Your mother, pressure of work, the accident."

"But not Nancy?"

"No, we must keep her out of it." Neither looked at the other.

"I'll take you to your room. Then I'll have to deal with the police and the press. Later on, we'll get you looked at by a doctor and, if you're well enough, tomorrow we can go home."

He helped her up, and they walked back into the lobby. Immediately, a man from the *Daily News* came up to Agatha and said, "Mrs. Christie."

"Yes," she answered, baffled by the crowd of people.

"Why did you come to Harrogate, Mrs. Christie?"

She looked at him, bewildered.

"My wife's not well," Archie interrupted. "Leave her alone. She doesn't know who she is. I'm not even sure she recognizes me."

Out of the crowd, Oscar Jones pushed forward, eager to be included in the drama.

"I'd just like to say it was a great pleasure to have met you."

"Thank you," she said. "May I introduce you to my brother?"

Oscar shook the Colonel's hand, while several more reporters fired questions.

"I can't answer you right now," Archie said.

"My wife has to rest. She needs medical attention."

McDowell guided the couple toward the staircase.

"We have a right to a few answers," one man said, managing to keep close to Christie despite McDowell's strong arm.

"All right," Archie said. He sought out the manager and asked whether he could use the Red Drawing Room for a press conference.

"Certainly, sir. It's at your disposal."

As Agatha turned toward the staircase, dazed and frightened by the fierce intrusion of the crowd, she saw Wally: "You haven't changed for dinner tonight," she said.

And he replied, "No, Mrs. Neele. That charade's played out."

"It's just begun," she said, and walked past him up the stairs.

Archie turned to follow her, saw Wally and recognized him.

"Good evening, Colonel Christie," Wally said amiably.

Archie ignored him. "Please get us upstairs!" he shouted to McDowell. "And tell them to leave us in peace."

Outside Room 182, he took Agatha's key and opened the door. "I'm going to deal with the press," he told her. "I'll see you later."

"What shall I do, Archie?"

"Lie down," he said, "rest. Just don't let anyone in."

He walked back to the top of the staircase, where McDowell stood guard. "I need to telephone," Archie said. "Somewhere private."

"How about the manager's office?"

"Good idea. In the meantime, perhaps you could get those press fellows rounded up."

"You're sure you want to talk to them, Colonel?"

"Best to put paid to all the nonsense, all the speculation."

They made their way down the stairs and across the lobby. The manager broke away from a group of reporters to whom he had been giving details of Mrs. Neele's behavior in Harrogate. "Anything I can do for you, Colonel?" he asked.

"Yes," Archie said, "I'd like to use your telephone. Also, I'd be grateful if you could give me a room, preferably next door to my wife. Just for the night. We'll be leaving in the morning for London."

The manager unlocked the door to his office. "Over here, Colonel," he said, indicating the telephone as if it were difficult to locate. "Anything else I can do for you?"

"Well, as a matter of fact, I believe my wife registered as Mrs. Teresa Neele. I'd rather not reveal that. She's not well, as you know. Had no idea what she was doing."

"I'm so sorry, sir, but I'm afraid it's too late. We've told the press already."

Archie picked up the receiver. "I presume this is a direct line?"

"Yes it is, Colonel," said the manager.

"Then I'd be obliged if you'd leave me alone."

Archie dialed the number of the Valencia Hotel and asked to speak to Nancy Neele. She came on the line sounding very loud and distraught.

"Archie! The most terrible thing happened. She tried to kill herself and I switched it on."

He interrupted. "Nancy, you must listen. I'm here, in Harrogate."

"Thank God! Where are you? I've been trying to telephone you for hours."

"Nancy, Agatha's here. Been here all the time. Lost her memory or something . . ."

He stopped, suddenly concerned for his girl. "What did you say happened?"

"It was Agatha. She tried to kill herself at the Baths. In a treatment. I walked in and she was behind a screen. She asked me to turn on the electricity, so I did. Archie, I had no idea who it was. She must have changed the current or something."

"Go on," he said. "When did this happen?"

"This morning."

"Are you sure it was her?"

"Yes, of course I am. This American rushed in and found us."

"What American, Nancy?"

"He's a short fellow, nice-looking, brown hair. He told me to get away as fast as I could. What are we going to do?"

"Dear God," he said under his breath.

"Archie, are you still there?"

"Did anyone see you?" he asked.

"I don't think so. This man covered her with a blanket and took her away in a taxi. She was half dead, you see."

"I'm listening, darling. Have you told anyone about this?"

"No, of course not."

"You mustn't tell a soul."

"Where are you?" she cried. "I need you!"

"Look, Nancy, I know who the American is. He's a journalist. He's probably already sent in the story. You have to leave Harrogate at once. Take a taxi and go to Leeds. Then get the morning train to London. Don't tell your aunt anything. The place is full of press and I've got to deal with them."

"I nearly killed her."

"Darling, you're all right. She didn't know what she was doing. Go home and I'll be in touch. I need your help."

"Please don't leave me."

"I have to protect you," he said. He put the receiver down slowly and examined his shaking hand with astonishment. Never before in his life, not flying under enemy fire, had he lost his nerve. Somehow he had to stop Wally Stanton's story. He put a call through to the *Globe-Enquirer*, asked to speak urgently to Lord Dintworth. When the assistant news editor refused to give him the proprietor's private number, Archie asked the man to contact Dintworth and get him to return the call. He gave the number of the Hydro and then hung up.

The Red Drawing-room was occupied by a dozen or more reporters. The manager had had the sofas and seating rearranged so that they faced three chairs drawn up against one wall.

Wally Stanton sat in the front row of these improvised stalls, his legs stretched out comfortably in front of him. When Archie walked into the room and sat down, flanked by Superintendent McDowell and the manager, he found himself staring directly at the columnist.

McDowell got up and told the press corps that since the Colonel was under the utmost pressure, they were to make their questions brief.

Local journalists had joined the London men, along with several residents of the hotel, and the paneled room was crowded to bursting point. Wally could detect the acrid scent of men on the hunt.

A reporter stood up. "Colonel Christie, when my colleague from the *Daily News* addressed your wife as Mrs. Christie, she answered 'yes.' Why did you say she was suffering from amnesia? Is she your wife?"

"The lady," Christie said, "is my wife. There is no question about her identity. But she's a sick woman. She doesn't know who she is, what is happening. She's definitely suffering from amnesia and probably concussion."

"Isn't that rather a clinical word to use—amnesia?"

"Eleven days have dropped out of her life," Archie continued, ignoring the question. "She has no recollection of events on the Friday or Saturday before she arrived in Harrogate."

Another man jumped up. "Could you tell me, sir . . ."

"So I'm taking her to London tomorrow to see doctors and specialists."

Archie glanced nervously down at Wally, who was leaning back in his chair, smoking. A reporter in the back row rose and read from a pad: " 'The disappearance seems to be a typical case of mental revenge on somebody who has hurt her. That's a quote, sir, from a doctor. Any comment?"

"Completely untrue," Archie said.

"You mean that the rumors about your marriage are unfounded?"

"I know of no rumors," Archie answered, wondering when Wally would make his move.

The first reporter stood up again. "You tell us your wife has lost her memory. Well, my editor has already spoken to a leading psychiatrist. The psychiatrist says that amnesiacs never take on another name. They're *desperate* to recall their own."

McDowell jumped up. "Mind your manners!"

"Mind my manners!" came the answer over the din of other voices in the room. "This isn't a classroom, officer!"

"Next question," McDowell boomed.

A small man stood up. "The guests tell me your wife behaved perfectly normally during her stay. The manager here said she joked with members of his staff. Could you comment?"

"I didn't say precisely that," said the manager.

"A sick woman doesn't usually get up and sing," somebody else said. "How do you explain that?"

Once more the competing voices drowned out the reply.

"Gentlemen!" Wally shouted. The noise died down a bit as several reporters waited to hear what Wally Stanton would ask. "I'd just like to say in answer to the last question that a person who has lost her memory may lose all recollection of identity without losing her memory for things like music. Any doctor would tell you that."

The room went silent. Archie watched, and he waited. He felt like a mouse given temporary respite by a sadistic cat. He noted that, as on the last occasion they had met, Wally Stanton wore a suit from a good tailor—and a social confidence unusual for an American.

A local man spoke up, more to impress his colleagues than to interrogate the Colonel. "She gave one of the guests a signed copy of a song called 'Angels Guard Thee.'"

The reporters broke out laughing. McDowell said, "Look, gentlemen, Colonel Christie's under great pressure. He's been very civil. I think you should finish your questions and let him return to his wife."

Christie was waiting for Wally. He wondered if he had already filed his exclusive story. And why hadn't Dintworth called back? "Are you sure your people will inform me if there are any telephone calls?" he whispered to the manager.

"Quite sure, Colonel. They've been given strict instructions."

An elderly man stood up. "We know you're under pressure, sir, but your wife doesn't seem . . . well, distressed. I mean, she has been responsible for the biggest search this country's ever made for a missing person. A number of people suspect it's some kind of publicity stunt."

"My wife is incapable of that kind of thing. She abhors publicity."

"Well, if she's a sick person, might not anything be possible?"

"All right, John," said the man on his left. "Don't push it. Look, Colonel, most of us are convinced it's not a publicity stunt. But quite frankly, Mrs. Christie's behavior during her stay here appears to have been very rational. Now tonight we saw her pick up a newspaper and look at her own photograph. You can't tell me she didn't recognize herself."

"Abnormal people do normal things when they're suffering from amnesia."

"Well, sir," said an old crime reporter, "even without her memory she seems to have eluded the whole police force of this country." There was more laughter.

"Gentlemen!" McDowell bellowed.

Another reporter spoke up. "The chambermaid says your wife must have spent a small fortune. Any idea where she got the money?"

"I don't know," Archie answered. "She drew on neither of our joint bank accounts." He looked at McDowell.

"This is outrageous!"

Wally got up slowly. He looked around. "I must say, fellas, I agree with the Colonel. You see, I found the lady." He looked behind him, took the attention of the room. "No question in my mind, Mrs. Christie just didn't know what she was up to. We should leave the whole matter in the Colonel's hands." He looked Archie in the eye. "Case closed, I'd say," he added, and sat down.

The room went quiet; the lust had suddenly gone out of the hunt.

Dintworth has silenced him, Archie thought to himself. He stood up and spoke stumblingly.

"Well, gentlemen, I'd like to express my thanks for the publicity you've already given to the facts of my wife's disappearance. Great credit"—he turned to McDowell—"is also due to the police of this country for their untiring and successful efforts . . ." He closed lamely. "In the matter."

"Thank you, Colonel," said McDowell. He turned to the reporters. "That's enough for to-night." Then Archie, followed by the Superintendent and the manager, walked out of the room.

The man next to Wally shook his head. "Sorry, Stanton, I think it's a voluntary disappearance, well staged. Anyway, where did she get all that cash?" Wally shrugged. Another man joined in. "Mr. Stanton's right you know, Bill. She must be sick or she'd have seemed more upset."

"Absolutely," Wally said, lighting another cigarette. "I think she's gone round the bend." Several other reporters had gathered around him.

"Anyway," he said, smiling broadly at his colleagues, "her husband wouldn't *lie*. He's a gentleman."

The Harrogate doctor called in to examine Agatha was comforting. He asked no questions.

"They think I've been suffering from amnesia," she told him.

He took his hand off her pulse and opened his case.

"*La belle indifférence,*" he said.

"I beg your pardon?"

"That's a medical description for loss of memory."

"A fine indifference," she said. "Or perhaps 'blithe' would be a better translation?"

"I wouldn't know, my dear. But when people suffer some unbearable pain, they block it out, simply cut out their past. Of course, I'm not a specialist, you know. Here's a sleeping draught for tonight. Mix it in a glass of water, and have a good rest, Mrs. Christie."

He closed his case and stood up.

"You'll be all right now."

"I hope so." She smiled. "Thank you for coming out to see me so late at night."

After the doctor left, she changed into her dressing gown and brushed her hair. Archie had returned. He was like a medicine that reduces a severe fever but leaves the patient feeling worse. The idea of recovery was to her vaguely offensive.

Yet, when Archie knocked and then entered her room, Agatha felt once again reassured—reassured because he was so evidently nervous.

"Look at this," she said, picking up a copy of the *Times*. She found the travel advertisement for Cannes and folded the newspaper so that he should see it.

"'City of flowers and refined sports.'" She smiled. "We could go there. Is golf refined?"

Christie smiled accommodatingly.

"Or South Africa again," she went on. "That would be lovely."

He sat down beside her where she lay on the bed. "You're looking much better."

She reached out her hand to touch his. "I miss you even when you're sitting here beside me."

Archie patted her hand. "You feel too much," he said.

It was his familiar rebuke. She wished he wouldn't pat her hand, pat it so gingerly. She smiled, feeling in control, till the anger in her rose like a boiling sauce. And yet she went on smiling, thinking she would not let go of him. That it was better to lower the heat, extinguish the anger, because she could face her own shame but not the hostility she felt for her husband.

"Do I think too much about myself?" she asked. "I could stop writing."

"I think that would be wise," he said, as if she had offered to give up chewing her nails in front of other people. "Especially," he added, "with all this publicity."

She saw him as he really was: the hackneyed line rattled around in her head. She tried out several other versions of it, while Archie went on about consulting doctors, telephoning her sister, arranging transportation for their departure.

The anger came shooting back. It felt ice cold. She said, "I tried to kill myself today. A journalist rescued me. So, you see, I don't think we're going to be able to avoid publicity."

"I know, I spoke to Nancy," Archie said. "I don't entirely understand, but I think it's going to be all right. That dreadful little man Stanton showed up at the press conference. Didn't ask any questions. Put on a show of support for me. Said the 'case was closed.' I've just spoken to his proprietor at the *Globe-Enquirer,* and asked him whether he had the story. He sounded rather apologetic. Said Stanton had phoned in a story about finding you. Dintworth asked me whether it was true you were suffering from a complete loss of memory. I told him that was perfectly accurate, and he was good enough to read the article to me. Odd thing is, there wasn't any mention of . . ."

"And what about Nancy?"

"Not a word. Course the fellow may try to sell it elsewhere. I particularly asked Dintworth about Nancy. Old friend, you know. He sounded rather embarrassed, asked me if it were true about the rumors. I denied them. Said I hoped he wasn't going to publish any, ah . . . false gossip."

Agatha kept quiet, hardly breathing.

"Well, what do you think?" he asked.

"I think that's very satisfactory." *Satisfactory* was a word Archie often used.

"Look, Agatha, you've been frightfully sick. Done something appalling."

"Yes, I know. It was appalling. I've been very unfair to you, caused you great distress." She spoke slowly without any inflection of feeling. "I'd like to apologize to you. Not just for the last eleven days, but for the last six months. Perhaps for the last few years."

"No need for that," he said. "Best thing we can do is bury the whole business as quickly as possible. And get you well," he added. "We're going to have to deal with the riffraff tomorrow, then pray God they leave us alone." He patted her hand once again. "The doctor thinks you'll be well enough to travel tomorrow morning. I told those press fellows we were going to London, to throw them off the scent. We'll change at Leeds for the Manchester train and then drive to Abney Hall. Your sister thinks you should stay with them for a while. You can rest there, get medical treatment, and no one can get near you. The place is like a fortress, I'd say."

"That seems a sensible idea," she said. "I'll be well and truly protected. And what will you do, Archie?"

"Well, I'll stay a few days in Cheshire with you, make sure you're on the mend. Then I'll have to get back to the office."

She nodded.

"I think I'm on the mend," she said.

He looked relieved. "Try and get some sleep." He stood up. "I'm in the room next door if—"

"If I should need you."

"That's right." He opened the door, then turned back to his wife.

"Thought I'd send silver pencils to the Hydro musicians, inscribed with our thanks."

She said nothing.

"Or perhaps cigarette cases," he went on. "What do you think?"

She continued looking at him without expression.

"You'd better get some sleep," he said. "Good night."

Chapter 12

By 6:00 A.M., seven of the most avid reporters were already waiting. An hour later, more than two dozen journalists and a handful of cameramen stood about on the grass verge outside the Hydro, looking up from time to time to the first-floor window of Room 182. A frost as hard as ice covered the spare winter garden, and the men from the press, their numbers increased from the previous night, stamped about, hugging themselves to keep warm.

They had done all there was to be done—photographed the hotel's doorman in his hunting coat, questioned Flora and Oscar, the members of the band, the porter, and the receptionist. Those who had just arrived had to make do with secondhand reports of the Colonel's press conference. Now they waited for the protagonist.

At about eight, Agatha drew the curtains of her bedroom window and stood looking out across the grounds. The reporters rushed forward and the cameramen jostled each other to get the best position to photograph the pale woman in the silk dressing gown who seemed unaware of the crowd below.

After a few minutes, Agatha walked away from the window and began to lay out her clothes in neat piles on the bed. She put on a fawn-colored dress and rang for Flora.

When the maid came, she asked whether the hotel could provide her with a suitcase. "Some boxes would do if you can't find a suitcase."

"I'll find you a suitcase, ma'am. Are you leaving this morning?"

"Yes, I am, Flora. I'm not well. My husband wants me to see doctors."

"I'll miss you, Mrs. Christie," the girl said. "I was always sure it was you. But I was wrong about that Mr. Baring. Thought you'd come up here to see him. An' he was a journalist all along."

Agatha smiled. "You can't really trust anyone, can you, Flora?" While she spoke, she emptied the contents of her dressing table into her small case.

"You're on your own in this life," said Flora ponderously.

Agatha laughed. "Not always, not if you take the risk."

"What risk, ma'am?"

"Take root in somebody else. A grafting operation. Doesn't always work, of course."

Flora looked uneasy.

"Sounds like gardening, doesn't it?" Agatha said, closing her valise.

"It does a bit, ma'am."

"Well, I'm a very keen gardener, Flora." She could see what the girl was thinking—that Mrs. Agatha Christie was sick in the head after all.

"Better get that suitcase, Flora, or we'll miss the train."

Five minutes later there was a knock on the door and Agatha opened it, expecting Flora. Wally walked in and shut the door behind him.

"You can't come in here," she said. "He's, he . . ." She waved her arms about nervously. "My husband's next door."

"I know where he is," Wally said. "Listen to me. You've got to get out, leave him."

Agatha stood still while Wally walked back and forth over the little square of Turkish carpet. "It won't be easy," he went on, "I know. You'll fall back a pace, then take two steps forward, but you can do it. And if you don't get rid of him," he rushed on, "I'm going to use that damn story."

She stopped him, her hands flailing about, extravagantly angry. "I'm not some sort of . . . of specimen to be analyzed. I'm rather sick of you and Evelyn telling me what to do and I'm sick of him and his . . . his silver pencils. He asked me if we should send silver cigarette cases *or* silver pencils to the musicians. Last night! How could he take me back! I'm sick of his propriety, and his secrets and . . . I don't like him!"

She stopped. She had said what had never even crossed her mind—that she didn't like her husband. The words seemed so much more brutal than if she'd said "I don't love him."

Wally saw she was ashamed. After a moment he said, "I could marry those hands."

She stood awkwardly, facing him.

"I think you're trying to be nice to me. You wouldn't marry my feet."

"No, but at least I can reach them."

She burst out laughing and sat down on the bed.

He couldn't take his eyes off her. He loved her. He loved her for her shyness, for the demands she made on life, for her blinkered, appalling romanticism, for her fight against the reprisals of childhood, for her violence . . . loved her because of her good sense in wanting to survive.

"Why didn't you use the story?" she asked.

"You know why I didn't use the story."

"What did your proprietor say?"

"He said he wasn't 'best pleased.' "

"Well, it was awfully decent of you," she said, looking embarrassed.

"You actually blushed."

"I'm shy."

"I know you're shy. I want to live with you."

She went on as if it were a game: "I'm too shy to have anything but intense relationships. You'd better go."

Wally shook his head. "No charade. Not this time." He leaned back on the chair.

She changed the subject. "What are you going to do now that this is over?"

"Usual stuff. I'm very good at it."

"Why don't you try something else?"

He smiled defensively.

"When you smile like that," she told him, looking at him directly, very confident, "you're covering up."

"Do you have to go back?" he asked.

"Of course I have to go back. To make amends. Until Archie's ready."

"You mean, until you're ready?"

She looked over her shoulder at the door. "You have to go."

Wally sat forward. "Listen, you never let me finish my speech. It goes on like this: 'He who does not really feel himself lost is without remission; that is to say, he never finds himself, never comes up against his own reality.'"

"You're lecturing me again," she said. "It's very good."

"Thought you'd be impressed. Somebody else wrote it. Some gloomy Dane. But I don't think you need that kind of stuff. You'll be all right."

He got up. "I'll always be there for you. If it gets bad, I'll come and hold you." He smiled his old practiced evasive smile. "Though not if you're soaking wet."

"Dearest friend," she said. "You'd better go now."

The word had got out that the Christies were taking the morning train to London. By the time the couple arrived at the station, a large crowd of townsfolk and many reporters were already waiting for them. The Harrogate police force had to form a cordon around the Christies for their protection.

Agatha held her husband's arm. Reporters

noted that she looked frightened by the surging crowd. As she arrived on the platform, a well-dressed man pushed violently past a young police-man and blocked Archie Christie's way.

"We're entitled to have an explanation!" he shouted. "Several thousand pounds of public money have been spent in this search."

"You won't get a penny from me," Archie said.

Superintendent McDowell helped Agatha board the train, while Archie stayed outside to face his angry opponent. "I pay rates and taxes," he said, "and the police are there for the benefit of the public. I didn't call them in. They were engi-neered into this business by the agitation."

"Your wife caused the agitation," a reporter called out. "Did she want the publicity?"

"That's a scurrilous suggestion. That's the last thing she would ever want. She's simply not well. Only this morning has she begun to realize who she is."

Several hundred people had managed to push past the ticket collector and get onto the platform. Among them was Evelyn, who succeeded in elbow-ing her way onto the train. Others followed her as she worked her way from carriage to carriage in search of Agatha. She saw her through the glass window of a reserved compartment. A policeman stood on guard. He said, "Sorry, ma'am, you can't go in there." But Agatha had seen her friend, jumped up, and came out into the corridor.

"How did you manage to get here, Evelyn?"

"Fought my way," she said. "I wanted to see you before you left. Had to find out whether . . ."

"It's all right. He's not going to use the story. I was going to telephone you."

"You're sure about that?"

"Yes, I am."

"Good. More than good. I'm sorry I was so . . ."

"You were lovely, Evelyn. You *are* lovely."

Evelyn took Agatha's hand. "What's going to happen?"

"I don't know what's going to happen." She smiled and added: "I'm suffering from *la belle indifférence.*"

The people who had managed to climb aboard had now spotted Agatha and begun to close in on her, despite the efforts of the police to keep them away. A woman guest from the Hydro grabbed hold of her hand and said, "I'd like to wish you good luck." Agatha thanked her while trying not to lose her friend, who was being pushed back by the crowd.

"*La belle* what?" Evelyn called over the head of an elderly lady.

"Too hard to explain," Agatha shouted back. "I'll write to you."

Outside, steam exploded from the funnel of the polished engine, and a porter walked the length of the platform checking that all the carriage doors were closed. Some reporters were already aboard, determined to follow the Christies to London. Others still pressed questions on Archie Christie, who stood on the steps of the door to his carriage.

"How do you account for the advertisement in the *Times?*"

"I have established that the advertisement was sent by my wife. She really thought she had come from South Africa and was anxious to get in touch with her relatives and friends."

"Well, what about the name she took, sir?"

"I can't explain that. We have a friend called Neele, but her name is Nancy Neele."

Wally stood at the back of the crowd of journalists, his hands in the pockets of his tweed coat.

"Among my wife's relatives," Archie went on, "there are some by the name of Teresa and it is possible that the two names occurred to her at once."

Agatha pushed down the window in the now empty corridor and leaned out, looking for Evelyn. She caught sight of her a few feet away and waved a small discreet wave. Quite suddenly she unfastened her yellow tulip brooch, still pinned to her coat lapel, and let it drop undramatically onto the platform. One or two people noticed that Evelyn pushed forward and picked it up. She was smiling triumphantly.

Archie Christie climbed up the steps, and the door was banged shut behind him. He leaned out of the corridor window a few feet away from where Agatha stood, and called down to the men below: "Make this clear. I do hope that from this time forward, all this publicity will cease and my wife will be allowed to rest and to recover so that she will be restored to normal health once more and be my companion throughout life."

Steam clouded the platform as the train began to move slowly out of the station and the group of reporters ran alongside, although the Colonel had already closed the window.

When the train had disappeared out of sight, Wally Stanton walked over to Evelyn Crawley.

"Wrong man," he said quietly. "Wrong questions. Wrong story."

She said, "That was decent of you, not to . . ."

"Wasn't it. What was it she dropped onto the platform, Evelyn?"

"Oh, some silly brooch, the one she always wore. Bit of rubbish, really. Here, you have it." She handed the yellow tulip to Wally. She began to laugh. "What a lark!"

"Yes, what a lark."

She looked at him. "I'm really sorry. You really liked her."

"Oh, I liked her," he said. And he smiled.

Two years later, in 1928, the Christies were divorced and Archibald Christie married Nancy Neele.

Four years later, in 1930, Agatha Christie married Max Mallowan and lived happily ever after.

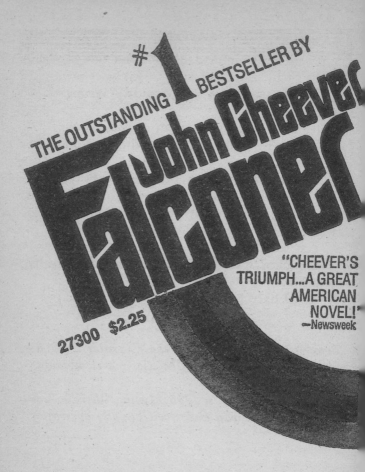

The game's afoot... and Holmes is giving chase!

Pulitzer Prize Winner
Carl Sagan's
THE DRAGONS OF EDEN

SPECULATIONS ON THE EVOLUTION OF HUMAN INTELLIGENCE

At last in paperback!
The entertaining and acclaimed bestseller
that takes us on a compelling voyage
inside the human brain. Combining
daring speculations and great fun,
The Dragons of Eden
is a masterpiece of scientific writing
for non-scientists.

Ⓑ Ballantine Books

26031/$2.25

LG-8